CANDY COATED PROMISES

Samantha Baca

Stone Creek Series

Chocolate Covered Mistletoe

Candy Coated Promises

Pumpkin Spiced Possibilites

Contents

One
Sheila

"I look ridiculous," I whined as I tossed my head back and turned away from the mirror. It was easily the tenth outfit I had tried on since I got to Brooke's house.

"You do not look ridiculous," she said sweetly, stepping to the side as she looked me over. "But if you don't like it then we'll keep looking. Tonight is supposed to be fun and I'm not letting you leave here until you feel sexy in whatever you decide to wear."

I pulled in a deep breath and shook my hands, trying to expel some of the nervous energy that was running through me.

"Why am I so nervous about tonight?" I asked dumbly, knowing full well why I was so nervous. It had only been a few hours since Parker had sauntered back into my life, looking delicious with his fitted jeans and a cream-colored turtleneck sweater. I felt like I was in some sort of romance novel where the absurdly good looking guy comes back to save the plain-Jane girl next door while he woos her with red roses and chocolates, making things far too fairy-tale to be real life. But yet, that was what happened. And as far as I knew, I wasn't part of some cheesy romance novel. Was I?

We had agreed to go our separate ways so the girls could get ready while the guys did whatever they were supposed to do. Both of them were gorgeous without having to try which was incredibly unfair as I stared at myself in a sparkly pink dress that my daughter had worn to Homecoming last year.

"I look like Pepto-Bismol." I glanced up and met Brooke's eyes in the mirror as she tried to look away before I saw the lines form on her face while she tried to keep from laughing.

"It's not funny," I joked as I turned around and swatted at her. "I look like something you take when you have the shits!"

"Okay, okay," Brooke laughed, holding her hands up in defense. "No need to get yourself all worked up. We'll find something a little less *pink*."

I rolled my eyes as she laughed her way back to her closet and started rummaging around.

"Did you bring those black skinny jeans?" she called out.

I looked around at the pile of clothes on the floor in front of me and on the chair beside me.

"Yeah, I brought two pairs. These ones that are incredibly comfortable, and these ones that are tighter and have fake leather down the side of them." I held both up for her to see as she walked back into the bedroom. She looked between both of them and then gave me a pointed look at the ones she thought I should wear. I turned my head and eyed them suspiciously as if they had somehow offended me.

"These ones?" I asked nervously, my face pulled up in a grimace. "Really?"

"Yes, really." She put her hand on her hip and tilted her head to the side, her expression softening for a quick second before she shook her head and reconsidered what she was going to say.

"But these fit really good, I already know what will look good with them," I countered, holding up the other pair for her to consider.

"Sheila Jane, those are the same pants that you wear to pull the weeds out front," she scolded.

"And?"

"And no one wants to dive into the garden looking for fresh flowers only to find dirt crusted weeds."

I wrinkled my nose in response and slowly put them down beside me. She walked over and smiled gently at me as she sat down on the bed across from me.

"It's Valentine's Day and Parker just drove all the way down from Nashville to come surprise you with chocolates and roses, while asking to take you out on a romantic date. You deserve to feel sexy and appreciated tonight. So put your weed pulling pants away and go put on the ones that are going to make him want to skip dinner and get straight to the dessert." She winked playfully.

"Is everything always a food analogy with you?" I teased as I got up and walked to the bathroom, pulling the door closed behind me while I changed.

"You know it!" she responded loudly as she laughed from the bedroom.

I pulled the dress up and over my head, sliding it back onto the hanger that was on the floor. I quickly hung it on the shower door before grabbing the pants from the counter. I bent down to step into them, stopping for a moment to look in the mirror, trying to accept that this was what Parker was going to see when he looked at me tonight. While we had already had sex once, that was a drunken one-night stand. Tonight was different. Everything was very deliberate and planned out which had me ready to crawl up the walls as my anxiety started to build.

My hands slowly moved across my stomach, tracing the outline of the stretch-marks that were proof of a body that had carried several kids. While people had always told me how lucky I was that I lost all of the baby weight from each pregnancy, no one knew how self-conscious I was about the way my body didn't actually *bounce back*. The beautiful thing about wearing clothes is that it hides the imperfections that we don't want anyone to see. My mind just couldn't wrap around the idea that if I wanted to be with Parker, then I would have to allow him to see mine.

I stared at my body for a few minutes longer while I traced the lace that ran along the top of my full breasts, matching the G-string panties that I was wearing. I desperately wanted to feel sexy, the way you're supposed to feel when you're wearing expensive lingerie that lifts and boosts all of your assets. But every time I tried to focus on something good about my body, I just kept thinking about how nervous I was to see how Parker would react.

"How's it going in there?" Brooke called, forcing me out of my trance. I bent down and grabbed the pants, pulling them on before looking around for a shirt to go with them.

"It's fine, but I didn't think about bringing a shirt that would go with these. I guess I have to wear the other ones after all," I sighed, feeling relieved.

Suddenly, the door opened and Brooke stood on the other side, holding out a shirt in her hand. She gave me a smug smile as she pushed her hand closer to me for me to take it. I looked her up and down, noticing that she had changed while I was in the bathroom. Her dark hair had been pulled up into a sleek ponytail that sat high on her head, showcasing a beautiful diamond necklace that hung just above her cleavage. She had on a simple black dress that was fitted in all of the right places, hugging her curves and enhancing the shape of her ass.

"You look incredible," I said with a smile.

"Thank you," she replied sweetly as she pushed the shirt at me again. "Now, get dressed so I can say the same about you."

I rolled my eyes and laughed, taking the shirt from her and holding it up in the air.

"Brooke, there are no sleeves on this thing!" I said as I turned it for her to see.

"Yeah, I know. But something tells me you'll be plenty warm without them."

I shook my head and pulled the spaghetti strap tank top over my head, pulling the bottom down to quickly hide my stretch marks. I noticed Brooke's gaze as she saw them, looking up to meet my eyes before I could turn away.

"You're beautiful, Sheila. Every single inch of you." Her voice was gentle, easing some of my anxiety. "You look like Ariel," she sighed.

I pulled my brows together and looked at her.

"Megan's friend?"

"What? No," she waved dismissively as if that was the most absurd thought in the world. "From The Little Mermaid." She smiled and walked off, leaving me alone with that piece of insightful information. I laughed and rolled my eyes.

I thought about what she had said when she saw my stretch marks. It wasn't the first time she had seen them, but it was the first time that I had felt that intimate connection with her that she was being honest about what she said. She wasn't saying it just to be nice because she was my friend.

I swallowed to force the tears away and turned to look at

myself in the mirror. The shirt was a sheer black fabric that was lightweight and flowy. It actually looked really good with the tight pants that I was adamant about not wanting to wear, though now I couldn't remember why. The outfit looked good and for a moment, I finally felt sexy. I was still taking in the outfit when Brooke came up and stood next to me, looking at my reflection in the mirror. She lifted two necklaces in the air before deciding on one and handing it to me.

It was a long, thin chain that had a single rose gold colored feather charm on it. I slid it over my head and gently laid it on my chest, admiring the way that it fit between my cleavage. I pressed my lips together and took a deep breath knowing that it was getting late and the boys would be on their way to pick us up soon.

We finished getting ready and took turns applying a new coat of lipstick before we heard a knock at the front door. I could feel the butterflies swarming through my stomach as I wrapped one of the curls around my finger anxiously, watching as the red hair twirled around it. I watched as Brooke walked over and opened the door, stepping to the side to let in Ryder and Parker. It felt surreal seeing him there, his jet-black hair glistening in the light as his emerald green eyes darkened when he saw me.

It felt just like a movie, everything completely perfect until the moment I had to move one foot in front of the other. It was too late to think of anything other than the sound I would make as I hit the floor when the four-inch heels I never wear decided to give me a harsh reality check. *Romance novel my ass* I thought on my way down.

8

Two
Parker

Sheila looked sexy in skin tight black pants that wrapped nicely around her petite frame as she came flying toward me, a sea of red flooding my view before she hit the floor with a loud thud. I had jumped forward, trying to catch her but I was a few seconds too late and too far to be able to stop the fall. There was a loud gasp beside me before the room went eerily quiet while we rushed over to make sure she was okay. I reached her first and dropped down onto my knees, lifting her hair out of her face to get a look at her.

"Sheila, are you okay?" I asked, panicked.

Her eyes slowly looked up at me under her eyelashes, the light blue color pulling me in. She started to laugh as she nodded yes and took my hand when I offered to help her up.

"Yes, I'm okay. Thank you," she giggled. "You'll learn

quickly that I have a love-hate relationship with gravity and I tend to spend a lot of time on my back, on the floor."

My eyebrows shot up as I pictured this, knowing that she hadn't realized the sexual innuendo that she had inadvertently laced into her words. I glanced over at Brooke and Ryder who were trying their best to hide their laughter, Brooke nestling her head into his shoulder to shield her face. Sheila looked around suspiciously between us, trying to figure out what everyone was laughing about. Her eyes narrowed at me for a second before turning to Brooke. Before she could look away, they locked eyes and Brooke lost it. Her laughter filled the room as Ryder and I joined in.

"What is so damn funny?" she demanded with her hand on her hip.

Brooke held her hand up to her mouth, trying to stop the laughter but couldn't. I waited to see who was going to be the one to tell her about her little wording snafu but when Ryder and Brooke refused to make eye contact, I knew they weren't giving in any time soon. Sheila looked up at me and gave me the cutest damn smile that made me want to pull her closer to me and kiss her.

"Your words might have gotten the better of you," I explained, waiting for her to put the pieces together on her own. She stood there for a few seconds, hand still on her hip when suddenly it clicked.

"You guys!" she squealed and looked back and forth between us. "You know what I meant," she sighed. "I am on my back on the floor because I fall a lot."

"You sure it has nothing to do with the four kids you have?" Brooke joked, quickly turning to hide her face in Ryder's shoulder before Sheila could look at her.

I let out a chuckle and reached out to hold Sheila's hand. It felt weird not knowing whether or not I should touch her or if she even wanted me to. We hadn't seen each other since the drunken night we shared on New Year's but I hoped that things would fall easily into place and we could enjoy our night together. She had seemed excited to see me earlier when I surprised her at *The Sweet Shop* but suddenly I was getting cold feet and second-guessing myself. She glanced down at my hand and smiled, placing hers in it before I gently squeezed it.

"You look beautiful tonight," I said quietly, pulling her attention to me.

"Thank you, you look quite handsome tonight as well." Her eyes slowly traveled down my body while mine took the opportunity to do the same.

I had been thinking about Sheila for weeks and had spent hours on the phone with Ryder trying to plan the perfect night for us. My goal was to come back to Stone Creek before today but some unexpected news had fallen into my lap at the last minute. This, in turn, derailed the majority of the plans I had made.

We had already missed our dinner reservation and the hotel confirmed that they had given our room away when we also missed check-in. Everything had quickly unraveled and I was left with the last box of chocolates and a bouquet of roses that I had to fight for in the drugstore. In all fairness, I didn't want to fight the little old lady but she didn't give me any other options after she kicked me in the shin and stole my bottle of wine. I had limped to the register with what was left of my dignity, paid for my stuff, and made my way over to surprise Sheila. I was still feeling nervous and anxious, unsure of whether she was going to like what I had planned for us or if she was going to think I was some pathetic loser who didn't know how to plan a proper date.

"Are you guys ready to go?" Ryder asked, breaking me out of my trance.

"Yeah," I said and rocked back on my heels. I looked over at Sheila and panic hit me when I saw her try to take a step and her ankle twisted as she started to fall again. This time I was able to reach out and catch her. She grabbed onto my arm, steadying herself as she looked down to see what happened.

"Stupid heel broke," she muttered, her hand reaching down to slip the shoe off one foot, then the other.

"It's okay, I have another pair you can borrow," Brooke offered and waved for Sheila to go with her. The girls disappeared into Brooke's bedroom while they found a new pair of shoes for her to wear.

"You excited for tonight?" Ryder asked once we were alone.

I rubbed my hands together and shook my head no. I was feeling plenty of things but excited wasn't one of them at the moment.

"Excited wouldn't be the word that I would use right now,"

I laughed. "Nervous, worried, stressed out—those are all appropriate words for what I'm feeling."

"Don't worry about it, everything will work out," he assured me. I looked at him wearily, not believing him for a second.

"Trust me," he winked as the girls made their way back into the living room. Sheila was pulling on her jacket, tossing her fiery red hair over her shoulder as she shrugged it on. I looked down and felt relieved that she was wearing shoes with a shorter, thicker heel this time. Even with the shorter, less sexy shoes, she still looked incredible and I couldn't take my eyes off of her.

"Okay, let's get going," Ryder said enthusiastically as he clapped his hands together and turned to open the door.

We all followed him outside, shivering in the cold as Brooke locked the door and we scurried to our cars. I walked to the passenger side and opened the door for Sheila, returning her warm smile as she slid inside and buckled her seatbelt. I rushed around to the driver's side, making sure I avoided any patches of ice before I opened the door and climbed inside. I glanced out of the corner of my eye a few times to see if she had noticed that we were following Brooke and Ryder. If she did, she didn't say anything or seem bothered.

A few minutes later I was pulling into the parking spot next to Ryder at the only restaurant that was open in Stone Creek tonight. The line of people waiting inside wound around the hostess station and butted up to the door. I groaned quietly under my breath when I thought about how long the wait was going to be and how our night was going to be wasted in this mess. I looked over when I noticed that Ryder and Brooke hadn't gotten out of the car yet either. He locked eyes with me and shook his head no before nodding for me to follow him.

I smiled nervously at Sheila as I put the car in reverse and followed Ryder out of the parking lot and down the street. I could see the curiosity and confusion on her face as we drove but I didn't bother trying to explain what was going on since I didn't have any idea myself. Soon we were parked outside of a pizza joint that was so empty it almost looked like it was closed. As we got out of the car, I looked at Ryder and pulled my eyebrows together, questioning what the hell he was doing. Another quick wink was all that I got from him before he wrapped his arm around Brooke's waist and led her inside. Sheila and I followed behind.

When we walked in, it looked like we had stepped into some sort of time travel dimension and were frozen in the nineties. The flooring was old and outdated as were the walls that desperately needed a fresh coat of paint. The lighting in the room was minimal and provided by some fluorescent lights that cast an ugly orange glow on everything they touched. Overhead an old Usher song was playing on the outdated speakers that hung in the corner of the lobby by the register. I looked around and saw that the room opened up into a larger room that was filled with booths along the walls and a few game tables in the middle of the room. One wall was reserved for arcade games and by the looks of it, they hadn't been updated since the nineties either.

"This place has the best pizza and is one of Stone Creek's hidden gems that only the real locals know about," Ryder said as he walked over to the counter and waited for someone to come.

"Are you sure they're open?" I asked with a heavy amount of doubt in my voice.

"We're always open, Sugar," a raspy voice said. An older woman who appeared to be in her seventies or eighties walked around the corner and stood behind the counter. Her black and gray speckled hair was pulled into a ponytail that frizzled out around her head. "One booth or two?" She reached down and grabbed a few menus while waiting for our answer.

We all looked at each other, unsure of whether we wanted to sit together or take separate booths. The place was empty aside from us which meant that we were likely to hear each other's conversation either way and part of me thought that it might feel weird to try to have any privacy with Sheila given that it wouldn't be private at all.

"One booth?" Ryder and I asked each other at the same time. Everyone laughed, which helped to ease some of the tension that was starting to build up inside of me. The woman nodded her head as she turned and walked off, leading us to our table. It was the biggest booth in the place and took up the corner which also made it more private, even though we didn't really need privacy at this point. I waited to see whether I should slide into the booth first, or if Sheila and Brooke wanted to sit on the inside. Thankfully I didn't have to ask before they both climbed inside and got situated.

The woman set the menus down on the middle of the table and stalked off, leaving us to look over them. I reached over and grabbed one, feeling silly when I noticed that no one else was bothering to look at it. I looked over at Ryder who was too busy whispering something in Brooke's ear to notice anything else.

"Do you already know what you want?" I asked Sheila.

"I'm not picky, I pretty much eat anything," she replied cheerfully. I loved that she was always so lighthearted and easy-going. Her energy was starting to wear off on me and I felt myself starting to relax more.

"We're sorry that this isn't a romantic dinner out ladies," Ryder said as he pulled away from Brooke's ear, leaving a blush on her face from whatever he had said. "But this place has beer and pizza—and more importantly, no line."

"It sounds great to me," Sheila smiled and reached over to pat my thigh under the table. I reached down and held onto her hand, thankful that she wasn't disappointed. It had been a while since I had been on a date with a woman but the last few had been pretty hard to impress which left me feeling a little desperate for this one to go right.

"You know me, I'm always up for pizza and beer," Brooke said happily.

A young, teenage girl with braces came out a few minutes later and took our order before rushing off to tell the older woman that the table in the back needed beer and she wasn't allowed to touch it. Sheila laughed and joked about how she reminded her of her daughter before looking over at me. I swallowed hard and looked away as I tried to force the anxiety away. There was a lot on my mind but I wasn't ready to unload any of it on Sheila right now. I needed time to process everything that had happened in the last twenty-four hours.

Thirty minutes later, a sizzling hot pepperoni pizza was delivered to our table along with two pitchers of beer. Ryder hadn't been lying, this place had some of the best pizza I had tasted as I chewed my bite that was too hot to be eaten. I forced it down and took a drink of beer, hoping the cold liquid would squelch the burning sensation from the pizza.

I waited a few minutes before taking another bite so it could cool down some. I lifted my beer to my lips and took a slow drink, watching Sheila as she looked around the table with a frown on her face. A few seconds later she lifted herself out of the booth and reached across, moving the napkins out of the way to find the shaker of crushed red peppers. Her eyes went wide with excitement as she sat back down and sprinkled them generously over her slice of pizza.

"You know those are hot, right?" I asked with a raised eyebrow.

"Mmhmm, just the way I like it," she replied, setting the shaker down before picking up her slice and taking a bite. She closed her eyes and let out a heavy sigh as she chewed, the whole thing looking sexier than it should have.

I leaned back against the soft, worn-out leather of the booth and watched her while I slowly drank my beer. She ate her pizza as if no one was watching, wiping her mouth with her fingers in between bites as she moaned and savored each piece. Suddenly, I felt her eyes on me as she noticed me staring at her. I felt a blush creep up my neck, knowing that I had been caught.

"Why aren't you eating your pizza?" she asked quietly, nodding at the untouched slice on my plate.

"It was too hot," I shrugged. "I was letting it cool down."

"It's always better when it's hot," she leaned closer to whisper, "And I'm not just talking about the pizza."

I watched her bring her slice up to her mouth and her lips parted as she slowly licked them before taking a bite. Her blue eyes darkened, sending her not-so-subtle message straight to my dick.

Three
Sheila

"I suck at pool," I joked as I bent down and attempted to line my pool stick up in a position that would hopefully hit a ball. Parker leaned back against a table, one ankle crossed over the other, as he held his pool stick beside him and watched me. Every few seconds I would catch him checking out my rack as I leaned forward, giving him a good view of the girls. I made a quick mental note to thank Brooke for loaning me the shirt.

"Here, let me help you," he offered as he pushed off from the table and set his pool stick down before walking over and standing beside me. I immediately felt the heat from his body as his chest pressed against mine when he leaned forward to help angle my arm in a better position. He slightly scooted forward, his groin lining up perfectly so I could feel the prominent outline of the bulge in his jeans. I held my breath as I waited for him to move again, my body hyper-aware of every touch. One hand reached forward and slid down my arm, wrapping over my hand to help guide the pool stick while the other hand was placed firmly on my lower back, just inches above my ass.

"Try that," he said softly as he slowly pulled away and walked to the side of me. I pulled in a deep breath and held it, forcing myself to focus on the ball and not on the way my body was still humming from his touch. His eyes were locked onto my every movement as I pulled my arm back and pushed the pool cue forward, excited when I saw the ball move across the pool table. I squealed with joy and looked up to find him smiling before he started clapping.

"Great shot." His voice was smooth and sexy, the nervousness I had seen in him earlier now replaced by the relaxed Parker I remembered from Christmas and New Year's. Maybe it was the few beers he had drank or maybe it was just us spending more time together. My nerves had finally calmed down too, thankfully.

"Well, I had a great teacher," I replied with a wink. "I'm sure it was a one-time-only thing."

"Nah, I'm sure you'll sink the next one and kick my ass this round."

It was our third round playing against each other and I hadn't won one yet.

I rolled my eyes playfully and walked around the table, trying to find an easy shot. I scanned the balls, trying to avoid the eight ball while trying to find a solid ball that wasn't stuck in between all of the stripes. I had sunk his balls so many times already, and not in a good way. It was a long shot but I spied a solid ball off to the corner of the pool table and knew that it wasn't the best decision but decided to go for it anyway.

I lined myself up and leaned forward to take the shot, watching as Parker's eyebrows raised in surprise when he saw what I was going to attempt. He turned his head to the side to cough out a laugh he was trying to hide before looking at me and shaking his head in disbelief. I pulled the cue back and pushed it forward, lowering my head as I watched it miss the ball I was aiming for and sink one of his instead. I closed my eyes and waited to look at him, knowing that he was going to give me shit for this.

When I opened my eyes, he was standing next to me, waiting for me to look at him. When I did, he looked from me to the table and back as a giant smile pulled across his face.

"You're not funny," I joked and swatted at his muscular chest. He caught my hand and pulled me close to him, wrapping his arms around me so I couldn't get away. I looked up from under my dark lashes and tried to keep myself from laughing.

"I didn't say anything," he teased playfully before lifting my chin with his finger. Once my head was lifted and I was fully looking at him, his smile grew wider as he said, "you really have a thing for my balls tonight, don't you?"

I felt the heat flush through my body, my cheeks burning from the blush.

"What can I say, you're just so good that women practically

throw themselves at you," I joked back. "Not just once, but twice. You must be quite the stud."

He laughed and leaned forward, planting a kiss on my lips.

"How's your ankle by the way?" he asked, his tone shifting from playful to concerned.

"It's fine. As I said, I fall a lot so my body is used to it." I tried to make light of it but it really had been killing me all night. I had tried to take the edge off with a couple of beers but wanted to make sure that I didn't have too many so we didn't end up having a repeat from New Year's Eve. Not that the sex was bad that night, I just wish I had been more sober to remember and enjoy all of it. There were a few parts that were unfortunately a blur. Like, the image of his black hair as it tickled my lower stomach while his face was buried between my legs. That was something I definitely wished I could remember in more detail.

"It's probably a good idea for you to get off of it soon, we can call this our last game if you want?"

"Yeah, that's fine with me." I glanced at the clock on the wall and noticed it was already after nine o'clock and knew it would be closing time soon. Ryder and Brooke were off on the other side of the room playing video games and making bets on what the loser would have to do when they got home later. I was a tiny bit jealous of how easy their relationship seemed to flow and how into each other they seemed to be. Then I reminded myself that Parker and I might be like that someday too but it was still too early in our relationship to have that level of comfort. If you counted the number of days we had physically spent together, it was barely a week and a half of us dating.

"Was there anything you wanted to do after this?" He asked shyly as he moved around the table, clearing the rest of the balls in a few effortless moves. I swallowed hard and froze, realizing that we were at that point where we had to decide if we were going to invite each other back to our place for the night. The kids were with my ex-husband, Rodney, and his girlfriend—possibly fiancé if everything went well—tonight so I had the house to myself. There was also the option to go back to his hotel room with him if he invited me.

"I have the house to myself," I blurted out nervously as I tapped my fingers against the table I was sitting at. "We can go there if you want to. Or not. I don't want you to feel pressured to do it." My face fell as the words came flying out of my mouth uncontrollably. "I don't mean *do it,* I meant if you wanted to come over and—"

"Sheila," he interrupted and pinned me with a look. "I would love to come over and hang out."

I nodded and slowly exhaled, hoping that the next batch of oxygen that I inhaled would at least make it to my brain. Brooke and Ryder finished their game and headed over to the pool table as Parker finished setting it up how we had originally found it.

"They're getting ready to close so we better get going," Ryder said, looking past me to Parker. I took the opportunity to sneak a glance at Brooke who was smiling mischievously at me before she looked me up and down and wiggled her eyebrows. I rolled my eyes and shook my head, feeling somewhat more relaxed now that they had joined us again. It was weird that even though Parker and I had already had sex, I felt like a nervous teenager who was stressing out about doing it for the first time.

"You ready?" Parker asked as we walked back to the booth and grabbed our coats. I nodded and smiled, trying to force any intelligent words to come out but failing in the process. We walked out and thanked the woman at the front before the cold air hit us and the door closed behind us. We said a quick goodbye to each other before we got in our separate cars and drove away. The closer we got to my house, the more nervous I was to invite him in.

Four
Parker

Sheila was quiet the entire car ride back to her place. I started to wonder if it would be better for me to go and let her have the time she needed so she would feel comfortable with having me there. I had spent plenty of time at her house the week between Christmas and New Year's but it was different now that we were a couple. Or at least I thought we were. I pulled into the driveway and looked at her before turning off the car or undoing my seat buckle.

"Are you sure about this? I don't want to make you uncomfortable in any way," I said, reaching across to gently squeeze her hand that was resting on her thigh.

"Yes, I'm sure," she said with a smile. "I'm sorry, I don't know why I feel so nervous tonight." She tried to force a smile but it never got close to reaching her eyes.

"We don't have to do anything that makes you nervous, Sheila. I respect you and we can go as slow as you want to. Okay?"

She nodded her head and smiled again, this time it was more of a smile than before. Once inside, I instantly remembered the time I had spent here with her, including the vague memories I had of New Year's Eve. That was a great night but I really regretted that we were drunk when it happened because I was pretty sure that it was definitely something that I wanted to remember every small detail. Part of me was hoping that we would have a chance to make some new memories tonight.

"Do you want something to drink?" she called from the kitchen while I made myself comfortable on the couch.

"Water is fine, thank you." I didn't want to have any alcohol in my system tonight so I could make sure that anything we did was with a clear head. The few beers I had at dinner were quickly out of my system after an hour or so and I had planned to keep myself in the right mindset tonight.

A few minutes later, Sheila came in with a glass of iced water in one hand and a glass of tea in the other. Her feet were bare after she kicked her shoes off the minute we walked inside. She set the drinks down on the coffee table in front of us and sat down beside me, looking unsure of what to do.

"Here, turn sideways," I said as I reached down and grabbed her feet, pulling them onto my lap as she scooted herself around on the couch. She looked confused until my hands gently started rubbing her foot and working the tender flesh along her arch. I shifted my position and turned slightly toward her so I could watch as her eyes fluttered closed and her head tilted back to rest against the corner of the cushion behind her. My thumbs rubbed along the inside of her foot, gently massaging as she quietly moaned in response.

I went to work on the other foot, kneading each spot and feeling my jeans pulling tighter around the hard-on I was getting from the sounds she was making. My hands slowly traveled up and started massaging her legs as I took the opportunity to check her out in the skin-tight pants while she wasn't looking. Everything about her was so damn sexy, I was already fighting the urge to keep my hands to myself. I had to remind myself that I was a nice guy who was giving her a massage because she deserved it and that I wasn't a dirty pervert who was giving her a massage as an excuse to touch her.

"God, that feels so good," she whimpered, her eyes still closed as her breathing started to change. I watched as her chest started to rise and fall more heavily, her back slightly arched against the couch. Was she getting as turned on by this as I was?

"Good, I'm glad. It's my job to make you feel good," I said lazily as I worked my way back down her leg, to her foot before I got carried away and tried to massage something else. Suddenly my throat was dry so I leaned forward and took a drink of water, hoping it would cool me off some.

"So then what's my job?" she teased playfully and opened her eyes to look at me.

"To sit back and enjoy it."

Our eyes locked and I knew that we both knew the true

meaning of my words and that it had nothing to do with the damn foot massage. She licked her lips and before I knew it she was across the couch and straddling me, her hands wound in my hair as her mouth planted on mine. I reached down and grabbed her ass, pulling her closer to me as my dick throbbed against the tightness of my jeans. I groaned as she sank lower, situating herself right on top of me as I imagined being inside of her while she rode me.

My hands roamed all over her body, desperate to touch her as hers pulled my hair before she pulled away from the kiss. We were both breathless as we paused for a second to look at each other before I leaned forward and started kissing her neck. She moaned and the feel of it in her throat against my lips nearly sent me over the edge. I loved that I was the reason she was making these sounds. I ran a hand up and over her breast, pausing for a second to feel the fullness of it before pulling her tank top down enough to free it from her bra. My dick twitched, spurring me on as I leaned forward and pulled her nipple into my mouth, my hands grabbing her ass as she ground her hips against me.

"Let's go to my bedroom," she panted breathlessly before pulling back and climbing off of me. I nodded and stood, thankful for the change in position as I followed her to the room. The lights were still off when she climbed onto the bed, only a trickle of light coming in from the hallway. I wanted to turn on every light there was, just so I could see her body and watch her face as I brought her to climax but something told me that she wanted to come in here for a reason and that reason was because it was dark.

I was unsure of how far things were going so I refrained

from undressing, aside from taking off my shoes, before climbing onto the bed next to her. There was a slight disappointment when I saw that she had fixed her shirt and that her breast was no longer out for me to enjoy but I didn't want to overstep by diving back in. I wanted her to make the moves and show me what she wanted and how far she wanted to go.

"You can come closer if you want to," she invited and patted the bed beside her. I smiled even though I wasn't sure she could see it and scooted over. I laid on my side, propping myself up on my elbow so I could look at her.

"You're gorgeous, you know that?" I reached over and gently caressed the side of her face. She was laying on her back, her head turned toward me.

"Thank you," she whispered. "I like the way you touch me, it's gentle but it feels incredible."

I slowly let my fingers slide down the length of her neck before teasing them along her collarbone. I kept my touch light as I ran a finger along the top of her breasts, gently tracing along the top of her bra.

"I like the sounds you make when I touch you," I said as I kept running my fingers along her body, making lazy circles on her stomach before getting to the top of her pants. "These pants are fucking sexy by the way. I honestly have had the hardest time not ripping them off of you all night," I admitted with a chuckle.

"Then maybe I should take them off?" She pulled her lower lip in between her teeth while she reached down and unbuttoned the top button before pulling the zipper down. I pulled my hand back and watched as she lifted her butt and pulled them down, freeing her legs before tossing them to the floor. She laid before me wearing nothing but the sheer black tank top and a black lace G-string. I tried to look up at her, to look her in her eyes, but I couldn't pull my attention away from her perfect body lying beside me, begging for me to touch it.

"Do you want me to put them back on?" she joked nervously when I didn't say anything. My head whipped up to hers and I felt myself blush, thankful that she couldn't see it.

"That is a *hell no*," I chuckled before reaching over and placing the palm of my hand on her flat stomach. "In fact, I was going to suggest that we take this off as well." I lifted the bottom of her shirt and felt the moment her body tensed beneath my hand. I leaned in closer and looked at her, trying to figure out what had caused the sudden shift in her mood.

"Are you okay?" I asked, making sure I hadn't accidentally crossed a line I wasn't aware of.

"Yeah, I just think that maybe I should leave it on. That's all."

I could still feel the tension in her voice and was concerned that something was wrong when she reached up and pulled me down on top of her. She brought her lips to mine and kissed me softly.

"But I do think we need to strip you of some of these clothes," she said playfully, tugging at my sweater as she pulled it up and over my head. I laughed and watched as her hands moved down to my belt, undoing it as her eyes slowly trailed across my stomach. She got so distracted that she hadn't realized that she was still staring at my body while my belt buckle hung loose in her hand.

"Did you want me to finish taking my pants off? You seem a little *distracted*," I teased. She pulled her hands away and I felt her eyes on me as I scooted off of the bed and stripped down to just my boxer briefs. I slowly climbed back onto the bed, hovering over her as she watched me. I lowered myself on top of her, making sure I didn't put my full weight as I adjusted myself.

She closed her eyes as my lips touched the side of her neck, kissing her softly while my hands ran along her sides and up to her breasts. I wanted tonight to be as special as possible and more importantly, I wanted to show her that she could trust me.

"Tonight is all about you, Sheila, just tell me what you want. Say the word and I'll give it to you," I whispered against her ear. Her fingers scratched along my back as her breathing quickened in response to my hand caressing her breast. "Tell me, what do you want, baby?"

"I want you," she whimpered, arching her back beneath me. "I want you inside of me, Parker. Fuck me, please."

I grunted as I reached across the bed to grab the condom I had pulled out of my wallet before tossing my pants to the floor. I quickly tore it open and pulled off my boxers before putting it on. In less than ten seconds I had her stripped of her panties and was sliding inside of her while she moaned my name and dug her nails into my back.

The sex was fucking fantastic and I wish I could have lasted for hours because that's how good it was. Her body melded perfectly into mine as we climaxed together. Everything about it was perfect until I looked down and saw that she was crying.

Five
Sheila

I tried to quickly wipe the tears away with the back of my hand before Parker could see them. I coughed to try to hide the sniffle when I felt his hand reach up and gently caress my cheek as he laid his face next to mine on the pillow.

"I'm so sorry, Sheila. I don't know what happened but I'm sorry that I've upset you," he whispered and pulled his hand away.

"You didn't do anything wrong. I'm just a mess today and didn't expect to have such an emotional response to us having sex. I'm the one who should be sorry. That was mind-blowing and by far, the best sex I've ever had, and I'm over here crying like a baby. Please don't think that I didn't enjoy it because I promise you that I did."

I felt my body start to shiver, the intensity of the emotions taking over. Parker reached down and grabbed the extra blanket that was laying at the foot of the bed and brought it up to cover me. I kept waiting for the moment when he would decide that this was too much emotional baggage and say goodbye before bolting out the door, never looking back. I wouldn't blame him, there was always a lot on my plate between my kids and my ex-husband. Not many people wanted to get involved in something that sometimes got down-right messy.

"You don't ever have to apologize to me for being emotional. I'm here if you need to talk but I understand if you don't want to. Just let me know how I can be there for you and what you need."

I felt his hand reach down and squeeze mine, a comforting reminder of what a sweet person he was.

"Thank you," I sighed and took a slow breath in, trying to clear my mind. "My ex-husband was supposed to propose to his girlfriend today and for whatever reason, it's getting to me."

I waited for a few minutes to see what his reaction to this news was before continuing. He nodded his head sympathetically and stayed silent.

"I don't have feelings for him and I haven't in a very long time. But something about him moving on with his life and asking her to marry him just gets under my skin. Maybe it's because she's barely older than our kids or maybe it's because they've barely been dating for six months. Either way, it just really bothers me that he is so ready to settle down with someone he barely knows when he wasn't willing to do that for his own family. He met her in

Nashville and thanks to their new relationship, he hasn't been around as much to see the kids and to take them on his weekends. It's a lot to unload on you, I know. I'm sorry, I just needed a minute to get it all off of my chest and thought it might be better for you to know what was happening."

"I get it, I'm kind of in a similar boat. My daughter has been seeing an older man for a couple of months now and won't listen to me or her mother about taking it slow and making sure that this is what she wants before she settles down. She's barely twenty-two years old, her life hasn't even started yet."

I turned my head to look at him as I propped myself up on my elbow.

"You have a daughter?" I was completely surprised by this information given he had never mentioned a daughter or family before this.

"Yeah, I had her when I was eighteen. Her mom and I dated when we were in high school and she got pregnant right before graduation. Her dad's work relocated him to Arkansas, so she went with her parents so they could help her with the baby while I went to college. We hadn't been dating long so the pregnancy was hard for both of us because neither of us knew each other well enough to have a child together. We stayed friends and I went to see her as often as I could but as Genevieve got older it got a lot harder for her to understand why I didn't live there with them. When her mom started dating Sean, it was even harder for her to understand the new family dynamics. I walked away to let him have the family life they needed for Genevieve's sake but I've regretted it every day for the last fifteen years."

"Wow, I had no idea," I said quietly, processing everything.

"I don't talk about it with a lot of people. Ryder doesn't even know about my family life and has no idea that I have a daughter. We hadn't talked until she showed up in Nashville a month ago and tracked me down. I've been trying to figure things out since then."

"And here I thought I was the one with a lot on my plate," I joked, hoping to lighten the mood between us.

"You definitely have a lot on your plate. I couldn't imagine what you're going through knowing that your ex-husband is ready to move on with someone so young. I don't think I would be okay with it if it was me."

"Rodney is a piece of work. Always has been. He's never been the one to do the right thing. Rather he chases down whatever the shiny new toy is that catches his eye. After he left, I had to figure out quickly how to pull myself together and be strong for my kids, and I've been doing that ever since. It's not unusual for him to spring crazy shit on me but even this is uncharacteristic for him. The man who couldn't commit to anything is all of a sudden desperate to commit to a woman he barely knows."

I chuckled and rolled my eyes, knowing it was too dark for him to see me. I felt bad bringing down the playful, fun vibe we had going early and wanted to find a way to create it again. For the first time in who knows how long, I had the night free to myself and didn't have to worry about the kids showing up unexpectedly.

"Do you want to go watch a movie or play a game?" I

offered, hoping he would say yes.

"I would love to but it's getting late and I have to head back to Nashville in the morning. Can I take a rain check?"

I tried to keep the disappointment out of my voice when I told him not to worry about it. We got up and dressed quickly in the dark before I walked him to the door. A gust of wind blew in as I opened the door and brought an icy chill along with it. I shivered as I leaned up on my tiptoes to kiss him before he rushed off to his car and drove away. I closed the door and locked it before allowing myself to sink to the floor in a pathetic, miserable puddle of salty tears and crushed emotions.

Six
Parker

The line at the coffee shop was long and wrapped around the building. I leaned forward and peered around the steering wheel to see how many cars were in front of me before deciding whether or not to say screw it and skip the coffee. The drive back to Nashville was long enough that I needed the coffee given that I hadn't been able to sleep well last night after I left Sheila's.

I hadn't planned to tell her about Genevieve but there was something about her that made me want to confide in her and talk to her about my problems. Maybe it was because we connected so well, or maybe it was because she had her fair share of things to deal with that I assumed she would be able to relate to what I was going through. I had planned to talk to Ryder about everything that had happened but it had been such a whirlwind that there hadn't been time.

Things had been busier than normal with trying to wrap everything up with the shop in Nashville before I could officially turn everything off and sell the building. Ryder had been great with helping me tie up loose ends but there was still a lot of work that I had to finish up. Things were going great and I was making a lot of progress until the day the doors opened and a young girl with jet-black hair and almond-shaped green eyes walked in, looking exactly like a female version of myself. My heart had skipped a beat as I stood there, speechless, staring at my daughter that I had only seen in pictures over the last fifteen years.

I had no warning from her mom, Amy, that she was coming to Nashville to look for me. Last I knew, she was still in Arkansas with her mom and Sean, along with her younger siblings. After sitting down and talking with Genevieve for a few hours, I learned that she had moved to Nashville a few years ago to go to college and was finishing up her degree when she found out that I lived there. Desperate to meet her real father, she tracked me down and we've kept in touch ever since.

The past month had been a complete blur with everything happening around me so fast. I had wanted to work on getting to know Sheila, even if it was a long-distance relationship to start with while wrapping things up in Nashville and getting things situated in Stone Creek. After Ryder moved, it didn't make sense for me to stick around in Nashville anymore. My family and I weren't close. I didn't have anyone to stay for. Until now. I had no idea how long Genevieve was planning to stay in Nashville but I found it getting harder and harder to want to leave, knowing that she would be there and might think that I was walking away from her again.

I was lost in thought as I pulled forward to the drive-thru window and the woman slid it open to give me my total. I passed her my credit card and took the coffee from her hand while she processed the payment. I forced a smile as she handed me back my card, along with the paper bag that had my freshly toasted bagel. The car slowly rolled forward to allow the car behind me to scoot up to the window while I worked on setting the coffee down in the cup holder next to me before driving off to get on the freeway.

It was still early in the morning, the sun barely peeking over the mountains as it made its grand entrance. I pulled the bagel out of the bag after I merged onto the freeway and set the cruise control. After I finished the last bite, I wiped my mouth and tossed the napkin into the empty cup holder beside me. I picked up the coffee and took a sip when my phone rang, immediately connecting it to the Bluetooth in the car. I glanced at the screen and saw Ryder's name, knowing that he was already on his way to work by now.

"It's true, the wicked never rests," I teased when I answered the call. I heard him chuckle on the other end.

"Yeah, not when you have a day filled with custom orders of *I'm sorry for missing Valentine's Day* chocolates and truffles. My phone was ringing off the hook last night with desperate men who needed a favor."

"It's a good thing Brooke knows what you do for a living or that could have gotten awkward…" I laughed.

"No kidding. But you know, for the right amount of money, I'm a pretty accommodating kind of guy."

"I'm just thankful that Brooke is stuck dealing with your nasty ass now and not me." I glanced over my shoulder, making sure the lane next to me was clear before switching lanes.

"So, how did it go last night with Sheila?" Ryder asked as I heard loud noises in the background.

"It was good, I enjoyed our time together."

I kept my answer short and vague, not ready to dive into the details of my own personal drama and definitely not one to gossip about anything she had told me. I figured if she wanted him to know, she would tell Brooke who would inevitably tell Ryder.

"Such a classy answer," he joked before cursing under his breath as another loud noise echoed in the background.

"Well, I am a classy gentleman. Unlike some people I know."

"Yeah, it's a good thing we balance this friendship out with your angelic ways and my deviant tendencies." I could imagine him winking as he said it, a total Ryder thing to say.

"Anyways, I just wanted to check in and see if there's anything that you need me to do on my end to help wrap up the deal in Nashville."

"Things should be all set this week and as far as I know, there's nothing on your end that I should need."

"Awesome. So when are you planning to tell Sheila that you're moving here? Brooke was just telling me that her neighbor is moving at the end of the month and plans to turn her house into a rental. Do you want me to get you some information on it?"

"Not yet," I muttered, trying to stall before having to come clean to him about why I couldn't just pack up and move out there yet.

"Not yet that you haven't told Sheila? Or not yet that you don't want me to get you the information?"

"Both." I blew out a breath and gripped the steering wheel tighter, thankful that there was very little traffic this early in the morning.

"Why? What's going on?" His tone was short and I could tell that he knew something was going on.

"It's nothing, I just need a little more time."

"Time for what? Just a few weeks ago you were practically ready to sell your soul to wrap up that deal so you could sell your house and move down here. What's changed since then?"

I waited a few minutes before responding, tapping my fingers against the leather on the steering wheel. This was it. The moment I would have to come clean and tell him about the secret that I had kept from him for the past ten years.

"My daughter."

Seven
Sheila

I woke up the next morning feeling like a damn train had run me over, rather disappointed that I was still here to feel the aftermath. My head was pounding, a combination of too much beer and not enough water, as well as dehydration from an excessive amount of crying. After Parker left, I had thought it was a good idea to stay up late and watch home videos of when the kids were little and Rodney and I were still together.

I spent the night thinking about our life together and all of the sacrifices that I had made over the years to make sure that the kids were happy and that I stayed on Rodney's good side. He was never abusive but immature beyond belief and had threatened to stop paying child support anytime he didn't get his way. It was constantly this balancing act of the kid's needs and Rodney's needs, never my own. I never worried about whether I was happy.

As I watched the videos, I got more and more depressed as I recognized how much I had changed each year. When the camera was on me and I knew that I was being videoed, I was always smiling and being the best mother that I could be. I hardly recognized the woman I was when the camera wasn't focused on me and I saw how tired and unhappy I really looked.

My body protested as I rolled over and climbed out of bed, the soreness from falling last night a quick reminder of how the evening started. I laughed out loud to myself, imagining what a klutz I looked like to Parker when I practically went flying into his arms. His face was etched with concern when he tried to catch me but couldn't and for a moment, I felt like someone other than Brooke and my kids cared about me. I felt seen and was no longer the invisible woman who worked her magic to make everyone else happy.

I wandered to the kitchen and started a pot of coffee knowing that I was going to need more than just one cup to get through the day. Sundays were supposed to be my hectic days of getting things ready for the next week and usually, I could delegate chores to the kids to lighten the load but they were still at their dad's. I was told that I could go get them this evening after they had supper, which meant that I had the day to myself.

While I desperately wanted to curl up on the couch and hide from the world and my problems, I knew that I was better off if I kept myself busy and got stuff down around the house. I always felt better when my to-do list was short and things were done so I didn't have to stress about them. After I cleaned out the fridge, tossed the leftovers that no one had bothered to eat, started a load of laundry, took the trash out, and vacuumed the house, I finally sat down and took a quick break.

It was after eleven and I imagined that Parker would be back in Nashville soon, though I had no idea what time he left. I had the urge to check in and make sure he was okay but decided to text Brooke instead and wait for Parker to reach out to me when he was ready. Things weren't necessarily awkward between us but they weren't the warm-fuzzy Hallmark feelings you see on TV either. We both unloaded a lot of personal issues onto each other before he left and went back to his hotel, texting to let me know he was there and thanking me for a wonderful evening. Regardless of where we might stand in our relationship, at least he was still a gentleman about it.

Brooke text back a few minutes later to confirm that she and Ryder had an incredible night together and were up until three this morning making love. I rolled my eyes and set my phone down, trying to push the jealous thoughts aside before responding to her. It wasn't her fault that she was happily in love while I was miserable and hopeless. I went to the laundry room and moved the wet clothes to the dryer before starting another load. As I walked back into the living room, I heard my phone ringing on the coffee table, excitement rushing through me that it was Parker calling me. My face scrunched in disappointment when I saw Brooke's name instead.

"Hey," I mumbled before plopping myself down onto the couch.

"Wow, who peed in your Cheerios this morning?"

"No one. I'm just cranky this morning." I looked down and picked at a loose thread hanging off of one of the throw pillows next to me.

"Why are you cranky? Did you guys not have a good time last night?"

"We did," I sighed and extended my legs out across the couch. "I'm just feeling cranky about stuff with Rodney and his new fiancé."

"Have you heard from the kids? Did he end up going through with it and asking her?"

"I have no idea. I haven't talked to them and I'm supposed to get them this evening. You know Rodney, if I mess up his day there will be hell to pay and I don't need that right now."

"He's such a dick," Brooke sighed. "I'm sorry that you're having a hard time with it. I know that you don't care about him or what he does but I imagine that it's hard to wrap your head around him proposing to a girl that's barely older than your kids."

"Yeah, and it's great that he's finally found *the one* but it's like a punch in the gut that we were never good enough for him to make that same kind of commitment. I guess I just expect too much from people."

"You always want to see the best in them and there's nothing wrong with that," she tried to reassure me. "How did things go with Parker? Did he have any *special news* to tell you?"

I froze for a minute and thought about what she just said. What did she mean by special news? He had told me about his secret daughter but had also said that Ryder didn't know about her. Had he talked to Ryder since last night and told him? It wasn't that unlikely that Ryder wouldn't tell Brooke something he had heard so I guess it made sense that she might know about it.

"Yeah, he told me last night," I said cautiously.

"What do you think? Isn't it great?" Her excitement radiated through the phone and tried to penetrate the thick layers of moodiness that were still surrounding me.

"I guess. I mean, I don't see how it impacts me."

Now I was really confused as to what Brooke was talking about.

"I would think that YOU of all people would be ecstatic about this. And it *absolutely* impacts you."

"Why? Because I have four kids? It's not like there's some special club that people with kids are part of."

"What are you talking about?" she asked, confused.

"Parker's *special news*," I said sarcastically.

"Sheila, what news are you talking about?" Her tone changed and I could tell that I was about to find out that there was more to Parker than I thought I knew.

"That depends, what are you talking about?" I wasn't ready to share his news about having a daughter with Brooke if he hadn't already told Ryder, but I had no idea what other news she could be talking about.

"Parker is wrapping up things in Nashville with the business he used to run with Ryder and once everything is finalized, he's selling his house and moving to Stone Creek."

I leaned forward and straightened on the couch, trying to process what she just said.

"What?"

"Parker is moving to Stone Creek to be with you and to help Ryder run the business side of things for us. Didn't he tell you?"

"No, I guess we never got that far in our conversation."

My mind was racing with other thoughts as Brooke went on about how her neighbor was moving soon and would be renting her house. Ryder was supposed to talk to Parker about getting information on it in case he wanted to jump on it right away as soon as it was available. She kept talking for a few minutes while I tried to force the bile down that was threatening to come up. For the life of me, I couldn't figure out why he wouldn't tell me himself that he was planning to move to Stone Creek. The only thing that I could think of was that maybe something had happened and he changed his mind. Something like a daughter that came back into his life out of nowhere.

Eight
Parker

"I already told you, I won't have the final offers until Monday morning so there's no use in drawing up the paperwork until the deal is closed and I decide which offer I'm going to take," I snapped into the phone at my realtor who had been pressing me all week long to accept one of the handfuls of offers that had come in after the recent open house. The week had been mind-numbingly dull as I tried to focus on the things that needed my attention. Instead, my mind kept wandering back to Sheila and the fact that I had barely talked to her since I left last weekend. I had debated packing a quick overnight bag and driving down to Stone Creek to see her but I wasn't sure whether she would want to see me after Ryder told me that Brooke had *accidentally* shared my little secret about moving there.

I assumed this was the reason she had been avoiding me and honestly, it was the reason I had also avoided reaching out to her. I knew that she deserved to hear about it from me instead of Brooke but there was nothing that I could do about that at this point. I had planned to tell Sheila that I was getting ready to move there soon but then my world was turned upside down so quickly that it made it hard to know what my next step was. The open house only added salt to the wound when Genevieve showed up unexpectedly and ran off before I could explain to her what was happening. It felt like every decision I made was the wrong one, and no matter how hard I tried, someone was bound to get hurt.

I finished the phone call and set my phone down on the kitchen island before opening the fridge and pulling out a bottle of water. I slid the barstool out and sat down, forcing myself to clear my mind and figure out my next step. There were only a handful of items left to finish wrapping up the sale of the business which was a relief. I reached over and picked up the pile of papers that I had printed earlier with each of the offers that I had received on the house. Each one was well above the asking price and a few were cash offers with the request to have the deal closed within thirty days. I looked around the house that was still spotless from the open house and tried to feel any sort of connection to it but couldn't.

Everything about the house was very clean, sleek, and modern. It had been a model home at one point and after I purchased it I didn't see the need to change much from how they had already decorated it. There was never the desire to change anything to make it feel cozier. I didn't hang any pictures on the wall or set any out on the fireplace mantle. I had been in this house for fifteen years though it still looked like no one had ever lived here.

I thought back to Sheila's house and the walls covered with pictures of the kids as they grew up. A handful of pictures were strategically placed around the house of other family members, but the majority of them were the kids. There was something about her house that made me feel like it was home but I couldn't figure out what it was. It wasn't the clutter and chaos of having four teenage kids with their stuff strewn about or the dishes piled up in the sink as they waited for their turn in the dishwasher. It wasn't the warm colors on the walls or the way you could sink into the couch from the wear and tear of a family that spent plenty of time on it. It was more than that and something that I had never known myself. Family.

Sadness crept over me as I thought back to my childhood and the house I grew up in. It wasn't much different than the one that I lived in now. Cold. Sterile. No pictures on the wall and no clutter around the house. The couch had been kept in almost perfect condition, only used when people would come by and my parents would attempt to entertain. Other than that my time was spent in my room studying, after making sure all of my chores had been completed properly. My free time consisted of guitar practice during specific hours and reading books that were selected by my parents. Neither of which were things that I personally enjoyed.

My phone vibrated on the table, pulling me out of the unhappy walk down memory lane. I picked up and saw a text message from Ryder, asking if I was planning to come down this weekend. I sucked in a deep breath and slowly exhaled before I responded no. I was frustrated with myself and knew that the best thing for me would be to go to Stone Creek and try to make things right with Sheila but I had no idea what to say to her until I knew what I was doing. Was I selling my house in Nashville and moving to Stone Creek or was I going to try to track down my daughter and stay in Nashville so I could make that relationship work?

After deciding that I wasn't going anywhere, I got up and grabbed a cold beer from the fridge. It had been a long week and I was thankful that it was finally Friday. Maybe being by myself this weekend would help clear my head and allow me to make the decisions that I didn't want to. I sat down on the couch and kicked my feet up on the coffee table while I flipped through the channels on the TV, looking for something to watch. I felt my phone vibrate against my thigh and grumbled, knowing that it would be Ryder giving me shit about not coming down to talk to Sheila. I found an old action movie and set the remote down before digging into my pocket to pull out my phone. I was pleasantly surprised when I saw that I had a text message from Sheila and not Ryder.

Sheila: Are you still alive?

I felt myself grinning like an idiot as my fingers quickly rushed to respond.

Me: Yes, I'm alive and well. How are you?

I waited impatiently, watching the dots move across the screen as she typed.

Sheila: I'm okay. I went by Rodney's to pick up the kids this afternoon and met his fiancé. I knew that she was young but I didn't expect her to be gorgeous. It hit me harder than I thought it would but I've been trying to keep myself distracted so the kids don't ask me what's wrong.

My stomach knotted as I read her text message. The thought that she was comparing herself to her ex-husband's new fiancé really ate at me. Instead of texting back, I shifted my position on the couch and held my phone up to my ear, waiting for her to answer.

"Hey," she said quietly. I glanced over at the clock and the wall, making sure it wasn't too late to be calling her. I couldn't imagine that the kids were going to bed at nine o'clock on a Friday night but what the hell did I know? It wasn't like I knew anything about raising kids or what time they were expected to go to bed at that age.

"Hi," I replied, a little too quickly. "Did I call too late? Or am I interrupting something?" I was suddenly nervous and second-guessing my rash decision.

"No, you're fine. I'm just feeling a little tired so I was resting in my room while the kids play video games in the living room."

"Are you okay?"

"Yeah, I'm good. Just a long day with an emotionally draining afternoon that carried over to a taxing night after I got into it with Oliver."

I had spent plenty of time with her four teenagers while I was there during their Christmas break and knew that Oliver tended to give her a harder time than any of the other kids. Maybe he thought it was his place as the oldest child? Or maybe it was just because that's what sixteen-year-old kids did?

"I'm sorry, that sounds rough." I didn't know what else to say and wasn't sure whether I should pry about what happened with Oliver.

"It is…" she sighed heavily. "So how did the open house go? Brooke said that Ryder told her that you had a handful of offers that were expected to come in from it."

I could hear the hesitation as she asked it, unsure of whether she should. Now was the time to man up and talk to her about what had happened, I owed her that.

"It went well, there have been several offers that have come in that were well over the asking price so now I'm just waiting for the rest to come by Monday morning, then I can try to make a decision."

"Try?"

I waited a minute before answering, hoping that I would be able to find the right way to tell her the real reason why I was reluctant to sell my house and move to Stone Creek.

"I'm not sure that I'm going through with selling it. Some things recently happened and I need to step back and figure out what's best for everyone at this point."

"Your daughter?"

I had expected to hear anger or resentment from her but instead, she sounded calm, like she understood what I was going through.

"Yeah," I paused and waited for the right words to come to

me. "I don't want to risk ruining my relationship with her by leaving. I hadn't had a chance to talk to her about it before she showed up when they were doing the open house. She was pretty upset about it and I haven't talked to her since. I've tried calling a couple of times but I get sent straight to voicemail."

"I'm sorry, that has to be hard. I don't blame you for taking the time to think through everything so you can be sure you made the right decision. As a parent, our children should always come first. Even if that means that you stay in Nashville."

"I'm the one who should be sorry," I apologized. "You should have heard about the move from me, not Brooke. I didn't want to tell you until I knew for sure that I was moving. After Genevieve showed up and told me that she was living in Nashville, it changed everything. After twenty-two years she came looking for me and I didn't want to let her down. I know what it feels like to have parents who are never there and I didn't want her to have that. When I walked away, her mom and I agreed that it was best for Genevieve to have a stable family life, even if that meant that I wasn't part of it."

"While I do wish you would have told me yourself, I'm not upset about what's happening. I get it, I really do."

I let out the breath I had been holding and allowed myself to relax on the couch. I felt silly about being so worried about how she would react to everything and regretted not talking to her about this sooner.

"You're an incredible woman, Sheila."

"I don't know about that but thank you."

"Trust me, you are," I assured her, knowing that she was still feeling down about meeting her ex's new fiancé. "And your ex is an idiot for ever letting you go."

"He has a new fiancé who is young and beautiful, I'm not sure that he would even care at this point."

"Trust me, it's his loss."

She was quiet on the other end for a few minutes and I had to pull my phone away to look at it to make sure we hadn't been disconnected.

"Is there anything that I can do to cheer you up?"

"I think I'm just going to make myself a cup of tea and head to bed. It's getting late anyway."

"Well, I hope you get some rest and maybe we can talk tomorrow?"

"Sure, that sounds nice. I have to drop the kids off at my mom's in the morning and then I'm free the rest of the day."

"Perfect, we shall talk tomorrow."

"Goodnight, Parker," she whispered sweetly.

"Goodnight, beautiful."

I hung up then grabbed my laptop from the other end of the coffee table and opened it to make a reservation at the hotel for tomorrow with an early check-in. After making sure it was booked I shut down the computer and made my way to bed. Tomorrow was going to be an early day and I didn't plan to waste one minute of it.

Nine
Sheila

"I don't know where your other shoe is, Sally, you need to go check in your room. Lord knows it's a disaster in there." I threw my hands up in the air in defeat before watching my youngest stalk away to go look for the shoe that was no doubt, wedged under something in her room. She was twelve going on eighteen with an attitude worse than that of her fifteen-year-old sister, Megan. Sometimes I wondered if the toddler years were better or worse than the teenage years. At least by this point they could all feed and bathe themselves so that had to count for something. Right?

I cringed as I heard the sound of things being tossed around in her room and knew that the temperamental teenager was about to reappear. I glanced behind me at the kitchen table, content to see that the other three kids were calm and eating their breakfast. My phone vibrated in my pocket, alerting me to a new text from Parker. It was short and asked me to meet him at the hotel in an hour. I glanced at the time and knew that it would be tight but I could make it after I dropped the kids off with my parents if they ever got around to finishing getting ready. I felt a mixture of nervousness and excitement to see him and found myself rereading the message to make sure I wasn't mistaken. It seemed too good to be true that he was here!

"I still can't find my shoe," Sally muttered as she slammed the one in her hand down on the kitchen table. I pulled my brows together and looked at her. A quick eye roll then the shoe was promptly removed from the table, along with a dramatic, heavy sigh.

"Why can't you wear one of the other pairs of shoes that you have?" I put my hand on my hip and waited, knowing that it was going to be a fight regardless of what I said. Unless I could magically make the shoe appear, nothing was going to make her happy.

"Because I told Jenny that I would wear these ones. She has some just like it and said she would wear hers and take me shopping today," she whined and looked down at the table.

I felt my stomach clench, hearing her talk about Rodney's new fiancé.

"Her name is *Jen,* not Jenny," Thomas corrected as he pushed the last of his cereal around in his bowl with his spoon.

"She said that I can call her Jenny if I want to." Sally jutted her chin out and pouted. Out of all of the kids, she and Thomas fought the most. They were three years apart and while he was a great big brother to her, he also gave her the hardest time for being the baby of the family.

"Okay, enough," I said, interrupting them. "Do you remember the last time you wore them?" I turned my attention to her, hoping to speed up this process before we ran out of time. She looked up at the ceiling as she tried to recall when it was. Megan sighed and pushed her bowl away before she got up and offered a sympathetic smile at me.

"Come on, I'll go help you look for them," she offered and walked down the hall to their bedroom.

Twenty minutes later and the kids were ready and piling in the car. I checked my purse to make sure I had my phone with me, just in case Parker called for any reason before I headed over to meet him at the hotel. After I dropped the kids off I took a few minutes to touch up my makeup in the car and apply a fresh coat of lipstick before making my way to go see him. Once I parked and got out, I pulled out my phone and checked the text message to confirm the room number before getting in the elevator. My fingers trembled as I slid them down the front of my pants, hoping to wipe away the sweat from my palms before I was back in Parker's arms. I couldn't remember the last time that I had butterflies and giggled at the thought.

My purse hung across my shoulder as I waited for the elevator. It was quiet this morning which wasn't unusual given we didn't have many out-of-town guests unless it was a holiday. The bell dinged and I waited for the doors to open before I stepped inside and pressed the button for the third floor. The elevator was older than the hotel itself after it was recently renovated, squeaking as it struggled to make its way up the first two floors. Once it reached the third floor the bell chimed again before the doors creaked open, allowing me to exit into the newly carpeted hallway.

I walked down the hall, checking the room numbers on the wall until I got close to his. As I approached the room he was supposed to be in, I could hear voices floating out through the door that wasn't shut all the way. I stopped and double-checked my phone, confirming that I was looking for room number 324. As I was looking up to see the number on the wall, I heard a woman's voice from inside the room. A shiver ran through me as I listened from the other side.

"I'm sorry that you had to find out that way. I wanted to be the one to tell you." Parker's voice echoed clearly through the door.

"You really hurt me by not telling me yourself. I thought this was something special for you too. If I would have known that it wasn't then I wouldn't have bothered coming all this way to talk to you about it."

The woman's voice pierced straight through to my heart and part of me wanted to run and run away while the other part needed to know who she was and what was happening. Was he seeing someone else and hadn't told me about it? We weren't official so it wasn't like he couldn't date other women if he wanted to, though he didn't seem like he was that type. But then again I had to find out from Brooke about his plans to move to Stone Creek so maybe I couldn't trust him to be fully open and honest with me or to tell me if he was seeing someone else.

I leaned closer to the door, desperate to hear more. I stood as close to the wall as possible, allowing it to support me while I balanced on my tiptoes. I was hoping that all of my yoga classes would pay off and that I would for once be graceful and not fall on my face.

"I know that I hurt you and I'm sorry. That was never my intention. I want this to work between us and I need your help to make that happen. Do you think you can give me another chance to make this right?"

My heart felt like it was shattering inside of my chest. What was happening? I felt my phone vibrating in my pocket, pulling my attention away from Parker and this mystery woman. I pulled it out and silently cursed Brooke when I saw her name flashing across the caller ID. The voices on the other side continued their conversation, however, it was now more muffled since I wasn't leaning against the door anymore. Just as I was about to resume my position, I lost my balance and stumbled against the door, forcing it to fly open.

Standing in front of me was Parker with a surprised look on his face. The woman had her back to me, nothing to tell me who she was other than long, black hair that came down to her ass. Her body was curvy and toned in jeans that looked like they were painted onto her. Everything after that felt like it happened in slow motion as she turned around to see what had happened, her hair flying over her shoulder dramatically like she was in a commercial for hair care products. The moment her green eyes landed on mine I felt my world crumble around me.

"Jen?" I asked in disbelief, looking between her and Parker.

"What are you doing here? Does Rodney know that you're here? Are you guys *sleeping* together?" My questions came out in rapid succession, not allowing either of them time to answer before I shook my head, turned, and stormed down the hallway. I was waiting impatiently at the elevator when I heard footsteps thumping down the hallway. I didn't have to look up to know that it was Parker.

My blood was boiling as my foot tapped angrily on the carpet. This fucking elevator was taking forever and I didn't have the time or patience to wait for it. Parker was only a few feet away from me and the elevator showed it was still on the seventh floor. I huffed out a heavy breath and walked over to the stairs, flinging the door open at the same time Parker caught up to me and grabbed the door.

"Sheila, wait," he said as he reached for my arm to stop me. I flung around and glared at him, the anger from a few minutes ago ready to boil over.

"Out of all the women in the world that you could be dating, you just had to go and find the one who is also fucking my ex-husband?" I knew that my words were harsh and my tone even harsher. I didn't care about that right now because this hurt deeper than anything else I had been through before, including when Rodney left us. Maybe this was different because I actually found myself falling for Parker and after all of these years I finally realized that I had never really loved Rodney. It didn't matter either way given that both of them were apparently in love with the same woman and that woman wasn't me.

"Please trust me when I say that there is absolutely NO

WAY in the world that I am sleeping with her." He let go of my arm and held his hands up in front of him.

I folded my arms across my chest and tilted my head, daring him to explain what was happening if he wasn't sleeping with her.

"Okay, then why is my ex's new fiancé in your hotel room?"

"Because that's my daughter, Genevieve," he said softly, stepping back and holding the door open for me to come back into the hallway.

I slowly walked forward, unsure that I had heard him correctly.

"What?" I practically whispered. My brain was struggling to process this information when I saw her walk up behind Parker and smile nervously at me.

"I thought your name was Jen?" I asked, looking past Parker to see her.

"Legally my name is Genevieve but my dad is the only one who calls me that. I've been going by Gen since middle school."

This was unbelievable. I stood there for the longest time just looking at them, unable to take my eyes off of the twins standing before me. I had no idea what her mom looked like but Genevieve was the spitting image of her father. They both shared the same jet-black hair and emerald green eyes, hers more prominent with the colors of makeup she was wearing. The jealousy that I had felt the moment I saw her at Rodney's house was somewhat gone now that I was associating her as the daughter of the man I possibly loved instead of the fiancé of the man that I once thought I loved.

"This is too much, I need to sit down," I mumbled to myself, looking around as if there would be a chair in the middle of the empty hallway.

"Why don't we go back to my room and we can all talk?" Parker suggested as he led me down the hallway by placing his hand on my lower back and guided me.

Once we were inside I chose a chair by the window and looked outside, watching the snow fall peacefully while waiting for someone else to start talking.

"I didn't mean for you to meet Genevieve this way, or for it to look like something else. When I texted you to meet me here, I had no idea that Genevieve was in Stone Creek. She had finally answered my call and when I told her that I was here for the weekend, she agreed to come meet me here," Parker explained, looking between us as Genevieve sat on the edge of the bed and folded her hands in her lap. "I didn't know that she was Rodney's fiancé until a few minutes before you got here. I had no idea why she would be in Stone Creek until she told me that she came down to spend the weekend with him and his kids."

I glanced over at her and took a few minutes to take her in. She was young and honestly not much older than my kids, granted she was twenty-two and my oldest was only sixteen. But there was something about her that screamed that she was still a teenager, not a woman ready to marry a man who was approaching forty and had four kids that she would be their stepmom.

"Does Rodney know that you're here?" I asked cautiously, knowing that he likely didn't. He had always been controlling when we were married and I doubted that he had changed much since then. Especially when his wife-to-be was a very beautiful young woman who could easily get any man she wanted. What the hell was she doing with him anyway? Suddenly, I wanted better for her and didn't even know her.

"No, he doesn't know that I'm here. I've been wanting to tell my dad that we're engaged and have him meet Rodney but he's been reluctant to come back to Nashville with me. I came down here to try to talk him into going back with me this weekend since the kids are with your parents. I figured if I pushed him hard enough, he would go. And he wouldn't have any excuses not to. But when I was on my way into town I had another call from my dad and knew that I needed to answer it before he started to worry about me. I asked if we could get together and talk this weekend, thinking he would still be in Nashville when I drug Rodney back with me, only he surprised me when he said he wasn't free because he was coming to Stone Creek."

"Wow," I sighed. "I still can't believe all of this. My ex-husband's fiancé is really my boyfriend's daughter." I shook my head in disbelief, feeling the flush on my cheeks when I realized that I had just called Parker my boyfriend for the first time. His eyes went wide at the same time Genevieve's did.

"I'm sorry—I don't know why I said that," I rushed the words out as quickly as I could. "We haven't decided what we are. Or what we aren't. I mean, we haven't officially labeled ourselves as anything—"

"I'm your boyfriend, Sheila," he said with a smile, walking over to where I was sitting. "That is unless you've changed your mind? I know this is a lot to take in."

I saw a smile spread across Genevieve's face as she watched us. I reached out and took his hand that he was offering and stood up. Wrapping my hands around his neck, I pulled him close and whispered, "I would love nothing more than to be your official girlfriend."

He pulled his head back and looked deep into my eyes before planting the sweetest kiss on my lips. Genevieve playfully cleared her throat to get our attention before the kiss turned into something more.

An hour later we were laughing and joking in Parker's hotel room and I realized just how amazing his daughter was. She was incredibly bright and full of fun, random facts. When she laughed, her eyes lit up the same way Parker's did and the lines at her eyes crinkled as well. She was a perfect combination of sweet and sassy with a touch of sarcasm that I'm sure her dad was thankful he had missed out on during her teen years. Lucky bastard.

Ten
Parker

When I woke up this morning I had planned to drive to Stone Creek and spend the weekend with Sheila, cheering her up from being down after meeting her ex's new fiancé. Little did I know that I would get a surprise visit from my daughter at my hotel room because she happened to be in Stone Creek herself, to talk to her new FIANCÉ. Who happened to be one of my least favorite people after getting to know Sheila. I also never saw it coming that Sheila would walk in on our conversation and immediately assume that I was sleeping with her ex's new fiancé. We were both blindsided when we made the connection that my daughter was marrying her ex-husband. If I didn't approve of her getting married before, I was definitely not approving of it now that I knew who the guy was. I was exhausted—mentally, physically, and somewhat emotionally after this morning and all of the information that had been unloaded in a short period of time.

I was thankful that Genevieve stuck around long enough for me to talk to her and Sheila at the same time. I needed to discuss the possibility of moving from Nashville to Stone Creek and the reasons why I couldn't make a decision yet. I had worried that it would be awkward and uncomfortable talking to both of them given that each of them was a reason for my inability to make a decision. I wanted to stay in Nashville for Genevieve and I wanted to move to Stone Creek for Sheila. Talking it out as a group was surprisingly easy and both of them understood the opposite side. Sheila wanted me to do what was right for my daughter and Genevieve wanted me to make the move to be with my girlfriend.

After a lengthy conversation about Genevieve and Rodney, I found out that she was debating whether to stay in Nashville or move back home to Arkansas with her mom, though she was having a hard time deciding because she didn't want to leave me. Her mom's health was declining and she wanted to be there for her. The problem was that Genevieve loved it in Tennessee and had no desire to move back home. She didn't want to put the burden of caring for an ailing parent on her younger siblings and Sean was working extra shifts to try to make ends meet since Amy couldn't work anymore.

When we asked her how Rodney felt about moving to Arkansas she confessed that she hadn't told him about her plans yet. She admitted that everything had happened so quickly and she had been caught up in the excitement of a new relationship that she didn't really think it through when she said yes to marrying him. I had watched Sheila's reaction to see if she would speak up and say something about it, knowing that things would also change for her and the kids if Rodney decided to move to Arkansas with

Genevieve. She didn't say anything and her expressions were pretty neutral so it was hard to tell what she thought about all of it. I knew that she had mentioned that she constantly had to stay on his good side so he didn't stop making his child support payments, but aside from that, I wondered if she would care if he left. She had confessed how hard he made things on her with the kids and that he had already started spending less time with them after he started dating Genevieve because he was constantly in Nashville with her.

I rolled over on the bed, careful not to wake Sheila up, and grabbed my phone from the nightstand. It was after ten o'clock and we hadn't left the room since she got here. We ordered room service for lunch after Genevieve left and spent the rest of the afternoon making love and talking. It felt good to be with her and suddenly I knew the answer to the question I had been stressing about for weeks. I was moving to Stone Creek to be with the woman I loved. I sent a quick text message to my realtor confirming that I would look over the final offers this weekend and have a decision for him by Monday morning. It felt good to know that things were finally moving in the right direction. Or so I thought.

Eleven
Sheila

I woke up to Parker's hand wrapped snugly around my waist, his breath warm against my shoulder while he slept snuggled against my back. Yesterday was a whirlwind of information to process but somehow I was feeling better about things today than I had been yesterday when I first got to the hotel. This nervousness had been eating away at me ever since Parker left after Valentine's Day last weekend and I couldn't help but wonder what it meant for our relationship. Or if we were even in one.

After spending the day with him and talking things out, everything felt like it was falling into place. We had said the slightly terrifying words out loud, that we were boyfriend and girlfriend. After Genevieve left, he told me that he was going to accept one of the offers on his house when he got back to town on Monday. From there he would work on getting everything moved to Stone Creek. His excitement about it quickly transferred to me and we spent the night making plans for all of the things we wanted to do when he got settled in. Of course, he still had to find a place in Stone Creek but that didn't stop us from daydreaming about our future together.

I had played around with the idea of having him move in with me since I knew there weren't a ton of places available in Stone Creek and Brooke's neighbor had already rented out their place. There were too many variables that I needed to consider before I dove off the deep end and opened my big mouth. First and foremost, how the kids would feel about it. They had gotten to know Parker over Christmas when he spent the holidays with us but they didn't know that we were seeing each other or that I had been keeping in touch with him since then. I felt guilty not telling them about it but I also didn't want to get their hopes up that something would happen with us and then let them down if things went south.

The sun crept through the sheer curtains, casting a warm glow in the room. I had no idea what time it was but I guessed that it was still early. My body desperately wanted to stretch and move around but I didn't want to wake Parker up since he sounded like he was sleeping so well. I closed my eyes and tried to fall back asleep, knowing that I wouldn't be able to. I was one of those people who once you're up, you're up. My phone vibrated on the nightstand beside me but it was just out of reach to where I couldn't get it without pulling away from him. While he might be able to stay sleeping if I did, I wasn't ready to not be in his arms. It felt safe and cozy and for the first time, I felt loved and wanted. I could stand holding onto this feeling a little while longer.

A few minutes went by before my phone vibrated again. Then again. I groaned silently, debating whether or not to leave my warm happy place. I glanced over and looked at it, willing it to stop.

"Just answer your phone," Parker mumbled against my shoulder, the stubble on his jaw tickling my skin as he slowly pulled away and rolled onto his back, locking his hands together above his head. The sheets shifted when I sat up and grabbed my phone, leaving his bare chest uncovered. My eyes wandered his body, taking in the smooth olive-toned skin that I wanted to run my tongue along. Even just laying there, his muscles were so well defined that he looked like he should be on the cover of a magazine promoting some sort of fitness routine. My phone started vibrating again but I made no effort to answer it as I stayed gazing at his perfect body, lost in thought.

"Sheila, you can eye-fuck me all day if you want to but that phone isn't going to stop ringing until you answer it." He opened one eye and looked at me with a raised eyebrow. I could feel the heat flush through my body as I blushed and looked away, forcing myself to redirect my attention to my phone. I looked at the caller ID and closed my eyes.

"It's Oliver, I need to take this real quick," I explained as I climbed out of bed and pulled the sheet around me, leaving him the blanket. He smiled smugly as he caught my eye, the blanket barely covering his dick that was already nice and hard, bulging under the covers. I subconsciously licked my lips and shook my head as I made my way to the bathroom and closed the door behind me. It was odd that Oliver was calling, especially this early in the morning, and I started to get a terrible feeling that something was wrong.

"Hey, Ollie, what's wrong?"

"Is it true?" His tone was sharp and I knew he was pissed off. He sounded just like his father when he was angry.

"Is what true? What's going on?" I racked my brain trying to figure out what was going on and what could possibly have him this upset first thing in the morning. He was fine when I dropped them off at my parent's house yesterday and when I checked in with the kids last night before bed.

"I heard dad on the phone this morning," he snapped out. "He said that you were dating Parker and that he's moving in with us. Is that true?"

I sat down on the edge of the bathtub and closed my eyes, allowing myself a minute to gather myself before speaking. Of course, Rodney would hear about my relationship with Parker from Genevieve but I didn't think he would be so quick to spin lies about it to the kids before I could talk to them.

"Honey, there's a lot that we're going to talk about later when we get home but I don't want you worrying about that right now. Okay?"

The other end was complete silence and I wondered if he hung up on me.

"Oliver?"

"Yeah," he sighed sarcastically.

"Just making sure you were still there," I said gently, trying not to piss him off any more than he already was.

"I'm still here. Unlike some people, I don't run off to meet my secret boyfriend and stay the night at their hotel."

"Excuse me?" I snapped, feeling my anger escalate quicker than I could try to control it. "You better take a minute and THINK before you say another word to me." I shook my head, catching my reflection in the mirror. Once I had better control, I started speaking again. "You do not talk to me like that ever again, do you understand me?"

"Yes ma'am," he muttered into the phone.

"Oliver," I warned.

"Yes. Ma'am." His voice was louder as he dramatically enunciated each word.

"You need to remember that you are *sixteen* years old. You're not an adult yet and you have absolutely no business putting your nose into my business. I will discuss my relationship with you when *I* am ready. Not the other way around. Do I make myself clear?"

"Yes, ma'am."

"Good. Then that's the end of this discussion until I decide that we will talk about it. Understood?"

"Understood."

I pushed the air out of my lungs that I had been holding in an attempt to not completely lose my cool with him. After I slowly exhaled I could feel myself getting calmer.

"Why was your dad there anyway?" I asked, suddenly confused about why Oliver was with Rodney when he was supposed to be with my parents.

"Dad came and got us last night from grandma's house. He said that it was supposed to be his week last week and that if you wanted the child support payment then you needed to let him have his time with us."

In an instant, my blood was boiling as my jaw clenched. He had some fucking nerve.

"Well, that was nice of him to call me and let me know," I replied sarcastically even though my frustration wasn't with Oliver. "Sorry, I didn't mean to take my frustration out on you."

"It's okay," he said quietly.

"Does your brother and sisters know about me and Parker?"

"I don't think so. They were still asleep. I had a headache so I had been up for a while but he didn't know that I was up. I had gotten out of bed and was going to get a glass of water when I heard him on the phone and stopped. He doesn't know that I heard him on the phone talking about it."

"What exactly did he say?" My curiosity got the best of me and I found that I needed to know what was said, even if it meant that I was asking my child to rat out their father.

"He said that Gen wanted him to move to Arkansas with her after they got married but she knew that he wouldn't be able to leave us kids. Then he said, 'she's moving her new boyfriend in with her at the end of the month and doesn't care about how it will affect the kids, so I can just move the kids with me to Arkansas and she won't be able to say anything about it.' I stopped listening after that and went back to my room."

My chest tightened at the thought of Rodney trying to move and take the kids with him to Arkansas. There was no way that I would let him move away with my kids but I also knew that he would immediately stop his child support payments if he didn't get his way. This had been a constant threat from him over the years and now I was kicking myself for not sitting down with a lawyer sooner to find out what the legal ramifications would be if he tried. I could take him to court and fight it but Oliver would be eighteen in a few years and I would stop getting his payment anyway. There was also the option of finding a second job to replace the missing child support or the option that I dreaded the most. Sell the house and move back home with my parents.

"Mom?" Oliver's voice jolted me and snapped me out of the depressing thoughts that were quickly multiplying.

"Yeah son?"

"I don't want to move to Arkansas. I want to stay here. With you."

"I know Ollie," I sighed. "Try not to worry about that right now, okay? We'll get everything situated soon but I guarantee that your dad isn't taking you kids anywhere without one hell of a fight from me. Okay?"

"Okay," he mumbled sadly, all of the anger that was there at the beginning of the call now gone.

"It'll be alright, I promise. Think about what you guys want for dinner tonight and we'll pick something up on our way home. Then we'll all sit down and talk about everything tonight as a family. Sound good?"

"Yeah, that sounds good."

"Alright, I'll see you tonight. And Ollie, please don't tell your siblings about any of this. It's best if we can all sit down and talk through things together. I don't want them to be stressed out or freaking out that they're moving before I have a chance to talk to your dad."

"I think it's too late for that. Dad just called all of us into the living room for a family meeting."

"I'll be there soon, just hold tight."

I sighed and hung up the phone. Today was not going the way I had thought it was an hour ago. I got dressed and walked out of the bathroom to find Parker sitting in bed, the blanket still barely covering him, while his fingers moved quickly across his phone. His eyes lit up when he saw me then changed when he noticed that I was dressed.

"Everything okay?"

"Um, no, not really." I thought about how to explain everything without getting into too much detail. "Apparently

Rodney knows about our relationship and is telling the kids that you're moving in with us by the end of the month. That is, if he doesn't take them with him when he moves to Arkansas with Genevieve."

I watched as the different emotions flashed across his face, starting with shock and ending with anger.

"Are you fucking serious?"

"Yup. That's Rodney for you." I walked over to the table where I had left my purse and picked it up. "I need to get going. I'm going to head over to Rodney's house and try to talk to him and the kids before things get too crazy."

"I thought the kids were with your parents?" He pulled his brows together.

"Yeah, me too. Turns out that he went by to get them last night because he decided he wanted his time with them after standing them up last week when he was supposed to have them."

"And your parents just let him take them?"

"I haven't talked to them yet but if I know him, he probably told them everything they needed to hear about how I knew he was picking them up and that I said it was okay. He's the best manipulator, as you can see."

"Why don't I come with you? Maybe I can help somehow?" He pulled the blankets off and climbed out of bed, bending over to pull on his boxers that were still laying on the floor.

"Thank you but I think it's best if I handle this by myself."

He stopped and turned around, a hurt look on his face.

"If you're sure that's what you want."

"It's never about what I want. It's about working around the landmine that is Rodney and keeping it from exploding. I've been working at keeping the peace for so long that anything new can set him off before I have a chance at calming him down."

"So how exactly do I fit into this picture? I'm your boyfriend but I'm not allowed to support you and stand up for you against your ex-husband who is going to be my future son-in-law?"

"I haven't had time to think through any of that yet," I explained desperately, feeling like I was on a downward slope with him now too. "I want you to be involved in things with the kids and me but I don't think this is the time to start. We barely just started seeing each other and now there are all of these other variables getting in the way. It's just too much right now."

He looked away and ran a hand down the scruff on his face.

"Okay," he blew out and looked down at the floor, his hands on his hips.

"Parker, I'm sorry. I didn't mean to hurt your feelings."

"You didn't. I just don't get why it's so hard for you to let someone else help you or try to be there for you. Rodney already knows about us and if he's going to be a dick to you and threaten to move to Arkansas with your kids, I should be able to stand up for you and help however I can. I get that our relationship is new but he's going to be part of my family anyway once he marries my daughter. Whether you like it or not, I'm still involved with this guy. I just wish you would trust me enough to let me try to help you."

"You don't know what kind of person he is, Parker. No one can help me," I said sadly. "I appreciate that you so desperately want to protect me and my kids but I haven't come this far and worked this hard to risk everything if things don't work out. It's all candy-coated promises."

"Candy-coated promises?" he repeated with a frown.

"They sound sweet but they're too good to be true."

"So what are you saying, Sheila?"

"Maybe we're rushing into things too fast. Maybe it's best if we slow down and take a break."

"A break?"

"From each other…," I whispered, not wanting to say the words even though I knew that I needed to. Parker didn't need to get caught up in my family drama and if I had any leverage against Rodney trying to pack up the kids and move them to Arkansas, I was going to have to walk away from the one person who had finally worked his way into my heart. I swallowed hard to try to keep the tears away that were threatening to spill over at any moment. With my purse on my shoulder and my head held high, I turned around and walked out, leaving a broken-hearted man to deal with the mess I had just created.

Twelve
Sheila

"There is NO WAY IN HELL that I am letting you move to Arkansas with my kids," I said assertively, leaning forward across the table as I pointed a finger in Rodney's direction. The kids were off in their rooms, likely listening to music and playing video games instead of doing their homework. Or eavesdropping through the walls if I knew them. Genevieve sat quietly beside Rodney, unable to look at me. I had been there for over an hour and we had been screaming at each other for the last forty-five minutes. I didn't believe in yelling or screaming to get what I wanted but when I got here my blood was already boiling, and I was on an emotional rollercoaster after everything that had happened in the last twenty-four hours.

"So, you can have some man you barely know move into your house while my kids live there, but I can't have them live in my house with my WIFE?" Rodney shouted back, slamming his fist down on the table, rattling the empty beer cans in the middle.

"I never said that Parker was moving in with me. Parker and I never even talked about it as an option so I have no idea where you got that information from but it's completely wrong. Parker and I *were* dating and he *was* planning to move here, but we never discussed him moving in with me."

"What do you mean you guys *were* dating? What happened?" Genevieve asked, finally jumping into the conversation.

"I mean that we broke up this morning when I realized that my life was filled with endless drama and that he deserved better than that," I snapped at her, barely taking my eyes off of Rodney to cast a glance at her. Her face fell as she lowered her head and folded her hands together in front of her on the table. I instantly felt bad for lashing out at her. This wasn't her fault and my frustration was getting the better of me.

"Well whether you're with pretty boy or not—doesn't make any difference. I bring in the money so that means that I get to decide where I live and whether to take the kids with me or not." He leaned back, the buttons of his flannel shirt pulling tight across his newly formed beer belly. He let out a loud belch and chuckled, not bothering to apologize for it. I turned my attention to Genevieve and tilted my head as if to ask her *really?* It seemed that he didn't care about his appearance now that he had found a young, beautiful woman who was willing to settle down with him.

"I appreciate the child support money that you pay for the kids but I assure you that I will find another way to replace that income. You will NOT threaten me again with child support. Those days are over."

He snorted and wiped at his nose with his finger before turning to look at Genevieve who looked like she would rather be anywhere other than here.

"I am not playing, Rodney. Threaten to take my kids from me one more time and it will be the last thing you do." I pinned him with a look and for the first time in my life, the anger in my eyes seemed to penetrate this thick skull. For a brief second, I saw a flash of realization that he knew that I wasn't playing by his rules anymore.

I don't know what came over me but I was finally feeling confident enough to stand up to him. Maybe it was my conversation with Parker this morning or the fact that I had felt like shit after I walked out and left him when he was only trying to help. When I thought about it, I had been a complete ass to completely disregard what he was saying and to refuse his help. I tried to picture how Rodney would have reacted when I walked in with my incredibly sexy, well-groomed boyfriend who looked like he could be a model. Compared to Rodney with his sandy-blonde hair that desperately needed to be cut and his clothes that were wrinkled and probably on day 4 of wearing, there was no doubt who the better man would have been in this room.

"Well, we'll just have to wait and see what the kids want to do. It's not up to you and never has been, you should know that by now." He pushed away from the table and walked over to the fridge, bringing another beer with him without offering anything to Genevieve or myself. I watched as she squirmed uncomfortably in her seat and I wished that I could pull her aside and have a talk with her to try to knock some sense into her before she went through with marrying him. I loved my children dearly and I would always be thankful that he gave them to me, however, I didn't want her to follow in my path. She had her whole future ahead of her and she shouldn't throw that away for someone like Rodney who would just let her.

"I really doubt that the kids are going to want to pack up and move in the middle of the school year and leave their friends. They've known the kids in town their whole life, Rodney, you know that. Oliver is starting his junior year in the fall and is already thinking about asking his girlfriend to prom. Megan made it on the junior varsity volleyball team as a sophomore—you can't just take that away from her. Thomas is finally adjusting to high school, it would be like starting over as a freshman in another school. Sally is graduating from eighth grade. These are all things that they're not going to want to miss and they shouldn't have to."

"Yeah, well, life ain't fair darlin'. Sometimes you just have to roll with the punches and go where the good Lord puts you. It ain't up to you or—"

"I don't want to marry you," Genevieve blurted out, interrupting him. Her eyes filled with panic as she looked up at him.

I felt my eyes bulge out of my head, turning to look at her at the same time Rodney's head whipped in her direction.

"What are you talking about?"

"I can't marry you, Rodney. I'm sorry. I just don't think that this is going to work for me and I wish I would have seen it sooner before I said yes. But I didn't and I'm sorry but I can't marry you." She rushed through her words, afraid to look at him when she finished.

I breathed out a breath of relief, thankful that she was a smart girl after all and that she wasn't making the same poor decisions that I had made all of my life. Rodney was a sweet talker which was probably the only reason she had ever started dating him. He could charm a used car salesman into giving him a car for free while thinking it was their idea.

"Gen, please don't do this," he begged as he turned in his seat to look at her. He reached across the table to hold her hands before she pulled away, out of his reach.

"You did this to her, didn't you?" he snapped at me as he swung back around to face me. "You filled her head with lies so she would leave me and you could get your way!"

I stared at him in disbelief and shook my head.

"I didn't say a damn thing to her about you. Maybe she just came to her senses and decided to walk away before she got caught up in all of your drama."

Gen stood up and took a deep breath before speaking.

"I grew up thinking that my biological dad didn't want anything to do with me because my mom never bothered to tell me anything different. When I would ask about him, she would blow me off or change the subject. After she started dating my stepdad, I would get in trouble if I asked about my real dad. I remembered him coming to visit a handful of times but never knew why he stopped. It wasn't until I found him a month ago and we had the chance to sit down and talk, that I realized why he hadn't been around. It was because he thought he was doing the right thing and giving me a better family life that wasn't complicated."

She paused for a minute and smiled at me, her hands trembling at her side. My heart hurt for her, hearing her speak about the childhood that she wished for with Parker.

"When we first started dating, things were fun and exciting. We went to concerts together and you took the time to ask me about school. Things were going really good and I didn't care about the age difference between us at first. Then I found out that you had an ex-wife and four kids that you hadn't told me about in the beginning. I should have known then that this wasn't the right relationship for me but I tried to ignore those feelings because I liked you so much. But now that I see how you treat Sheila, the mother of your children, I can't look away from that. Nor can I look away from the fact that you care more about your own happiness than you do about what would make your kids happy."

Rodney's face fell and for a moment I wondered if she had actually gotten through to him.

"So, you're saying that if I treat Sheila better and *try* to do what makes my kids happy, you'll give me another chance?"

I looked down and pretended to be busy with my phone to

avoid the awkward silence that was now lingering in the room.

"No, Rodney. It means that I've already seen the real side of you and I want to be with someone who wants to put his children first without it being a condition of the relationship. I have my own issues with an absent father in my life, I will not be involved in a relationship that creates those issues for anyone else."

I felt my chest well up with pride, amazed by how wonderful of a person she was. I could feel her gaze on me and smiled back at her.

"Well, then I guess it's settled that the kids and I aren't moving to Arkansas. You get your way, like always," Rodney muttered, looking down at the table as he spun the empty beer can in his hand.

"Like I've told you before, it's never about getting my way. It's about doing what's best for our children, Rodney. This isn't a game to see who they like better between the two of us, it's about making sure we work together to be a solid team that puts their best interests above everything else."

"Whatever you say," he sighed before he pushed his chair back and walked away.

"I'm sorry you had to be here for that, I can imagine it was uncomfortable for you," Gen apologized once we were alone.

"You don't ever need to apologize for speaking up for what you want," I assured her. "I'm proud of you. Not many people can stand up for themselves and know what they want out of life."

She grinned nervously, rubbing her hands together.

"I was so scared, I've never done anything like that before in my life." Her eyes lit up with excitement. "I felt in control and for once, I didn't feel like anyone was treating me like a child. It's such an amazing feeling, like I feel totally unstoppable right now. I should call my dad and sit down to have the talk he's been wanting to have."

"Sounds like a good idea." I stood up and pushed my chair under the table. She was already calling Parker when I walked down the hall and knocked on the kids' doors, letting them know it was time to go. When I turned the corner to go into the living room, I ran right into Genevieve.

"Sorry," I laughed and stepped out of the way. "I'm like a magnet for running into people."

"Same here, I can easily trip over air," she joked.

"Were you able to get in touch with your dad?" I asked, desperate for any information on Parker since I hadn't talked to him after I broke things off between us.

"He didn't answer. I left a voicemail but I'm guessing he's already on the road back to Nashville."

I offered a half-smile, unable to force my mouth to commit to a real one.

"I'm sorry that you guys broke up. I hope all of this wasn't the reason for it." She gestured to the air around us and I knew that she was talking about her relationship with Rodney.

I sucked in a shaky breath, unsure of whether I wanted to get into the details of my relationship with Parker with his daughter. I was already growing pretty fond of her in such a short time but needed to remember that there might need to be some boundaries between us if things did end up working between her dad and me.

"It's just the usual relationship stuff," I said dismissively as I heard the kids coming down the hall. "We're going to grab a pizza and head back to my house, do you want to join us?"

Sally's face lit up when she heard the invite and started bouncing up and down excitedly while begging Gen to say yes.

"Sure, I would love to." Gen smiled and took Sally's hand as they walked out to the car. I knew that sooner or later we would need to sit down and tell the kids that Rodney and Gen had broken up but for now, everyone was happy and that was how I planned to leave it.

Thirteen
Parker

Growing up in a house with parents who were never there, physically or emotionally- left a longing inside of me that I had tried to ignore for years. I pushed myself through life, always chasing after the next goal, feeling success with every achievement. It wasn't until I met Sheila and I had a glimpse into her family life that I realized that the one thing I had been longing for and was never able to fulfill was the feeling of love and acceptance from my family. My parents told me they were proud of me a handful of times in my life, but I couldn't remember the last time that they said they loved me. When I was a teenager, I sat down one day after school and asked them why we didn't say we loved each other. It seemed so odd because all of my friends did it with their families so why didn't we do it? Their answer was that only petty people who had nothing else in life felt the need to validate their feelings with words.

I decided to head back to Nashville after Sheila left. My mind was still trying to process everything, which explained why my knuckles were white as my fingers clutched the steering wheel angrily, the car accelerating past one hundred. I knew that I should slow down and focus on the road instead of obsessing over every tiny detail about our fight before she decided we needed to take a break. I guess you couldn't really call it a fight. I asked her to let me in and wanted to support her and she shut me out before she broke up with me.

The sky was alarmingly white with the threat of a major snowstorm, just like the weatherman had promised on the radio when I got into the car. I hoped that I would be able to pass through before it started. I leaned forward against the steering wheel and glanced up, confirming that I was about to drive through the thick of it. The snow started to come down in heavy sheets of thick, white flakes, and within a few minutes, I could barely see a few feet in front of me. I slowly released my foot from the gas, knowing better than to try braking and risk losing control of the car. The outside temperature on the dashboard showed twenty-four degrees which guaranteed there was a layer of ice already on the road given how much precipitation was in the air.

I continued to grip the steering wheel with both hands, keeping my eyes on the road while focusing my attention on my surroundings. There were a few other cars that were in front of me before we got into the storm but I had no idea how far ahead they were now. I imagined they had slowed down long before I thought to. The chill from outside was forcing its way in, sending a shiver through me despite the heavy jacket I was wearing. I reached down to turn the heater on full blast. All of a sudden, a blast of cold air shot out of the vents, startling me. I looked down to make sure the knob was turned to heat instead of cold, knowing that I couldn't afford to take my eyes off the road for even a second in this storm.

After I adjusted the knob, which must have accidentally been bumped recently, I looked up and held on tight to the steering wheel as the back end of a semi-truck came swinging right into the front end of my car. The last thing I heard was the sound of metal crunching and glass shattering around me.

Fourteen
Sheila

Three large pepperoni pizzas and four two-liters of soda later, the kids and I were stretched out in the living room. The movie we had been watching had ended, but we were all too full to bother with getting up to get the remote to change it from the six o'clock news. A red bar ran along the bottom of the screen with a series of weather-related warnings for the snowstorm that was supposed to be hitting Stone Creek this evening. I thought back to what Gen had said earlier and hoped that Parker hadn't tried to make it back to Nashville in this storm. Maybe he was in the shower or out with Ryder? Anything would be better than him attempting to drive a deserted stretch of highway in a storm that was predicted to be one of the deadliest storms in over a decade.

The screen changed and a man wearing a blazer that was two sizes too small started moving around in front of the green screen that was laid out with updates on where the storm had already dropped a few feet of snow and where it was headed next. I leaned forward, trying to see what the orange-colored box meant that stretched over Stone Creek, all the way to Nashville. Fifteen feet of snow was expected to fall before midnight which meant that no one was getting in or out of Stone Creek for a while. It also meant that if anyone was already trying to drive through this, they were likely stuck and stranded for a while.

The newscast switched back over to the regular anchor who was now giving travel safety tips for those who had to go anywhere within the city. While they discouraged anyone from driving in this, they also had due diligence to educate the viewers on making sure they had the essentials in their car, just in case. As they went down the list of blankets, bottles of water, flashlights, and batteries, I picked up my phone, hoping Parker would have reached out to me to let me know where he was. I knew that he didn't owe it to me and that it was beyond unlikely that I would hear from him, but I was desperate to know that he was safe.

"Have you heard from your dad?" I asked Gen as a commercial for teeth whitening came on. I didn't want to miss the news, just in case there was any useful information that she could pass along once she talked to him.

She shook her head no, picking her phone up to try again.

"It rings and goes to voicemail. He hasn't answered any of my text messages either."

I nodded, not wanting to alarm the kids by talking about how worried I was that he might have gotten caught in the snowstorm. We didn't know where he was or why he wasn't answering his phone, but the last thing I wanted to do was worry the kids that something bad had happened. I sent a couple of silent prayers up before I got up and walked into the kitchen, pacing back and forth while I waited for him to pick up.

The sound of the beep was annoyingly loud in my ear as if it was a direct sign of him rejecting me by refusing my call. I knew it was silly to assume that he had seen me calling and chose to ignore it because he was still mad at me, especially since he hadn't answered any of Gen's calls and he wasn't mad at her. A feeling of dread ate away at me as I started to consider that something might actually be wrong and that I wasn't just imagining it.

I waited a few minutes before sending a quick text, letting him know that I was just checking in to make sure he was okay because of the storm that was supposed to hit before he got back to Nashville. My fingers trembled as I pushed send, the anxiety starting to build inside. I chewed my nail while I watched the confirmation pop up that the message was delivered and waited a few more minutes for it to show read. Suddenly, my phone started to vibrate in my hand, the excitement quickly replaced with disappointment when I saw Brooke's name on the screen and not Parker's.

"Hey," I tried to sound as cheery as possible.

"Well don't you sound as happy as a clam? What's wrong?"

"Nothing," I lied. I wasn't ready to get into the details of my day with her just yet. Between breaking up with Parker and dealing with Rodney who was also just dumped by Gen, it was a lot to go over and required more energy than I had. "I just had a long day and had to deal with Rodney."

"Oh, that explains the bad mood," she said sympathetically, knowing my past with him well enough to not have to ask for more information.

"What's up?" I asked as I cleaned up the kid's mess from the kitchen table so I didn't have to do it later.

"I was wondering if Parker was there with you? Ryder has been trying to reach him but he's not answering his calls or texts."

My stomach dropped along with the pile of empty pizza boxes that were in my hand before I could take them out to the trash in the garage. Something was definitely wrong if none of us were able to reach him.

"Sheila? Did you hear me?" Brooke's voice was louder on the other end, forcing me to focus instead of going down the rabbit hole of tragic what-ifs.

"Yeah, I heard you. No, he's not here and I haven't heard from him either."

"Is everything okay? Did you guys have a fight?"

"I don't want to get into it now but we broke up this morning," I sighed heavily as I bent down to pick up the boxes.

"Sheila, why didn't you call me?" Her voice was surprisingly empathetic, void of any judgment.

"Because the day has been long and I haven't had a chance."

"Okay, I get it. I won't pry. But if you hear from him, will you please let me know so Ryder will stop worrying?"

"Yeah, I'll let you know. I'm sure Gen will hear from him before I will so I'll keep you posted. So far he hasn't answered her calls or texts either."

"Who's Gen?"

Suddenly it occurred to me that Brooke and Ryder didn't know about Parker's daughter because he had been planning to tell them this weekend before everything got so crazy. We had talked about meeting them for lunch today, but that was before I broke his heart and left before breakfast. It was still hard to believe that I had barely found out about Genevieve a week ago and that it had barely been twenty-four hours since I found out that she was also the same person as Rodney's, now former, fiancé. There was a lot to unpack and I felt uncomfortable telling Brooke all of Parker's secrets over the phone when we should have been more concerned with where he was.

I took a slow, steady breath in and tried to think as quickly as I could. I was a terrible liar but this was a time when I needed to come up with something and fast.

"Sheila—who is Gen?" Brooke asked again, more aggressively this time.

"She's his daughter," I breathed out.

"What?!"

The phone was silent for a few minutes before she came back on the line.

"How does Parker have a daughter that no one knew about? Including his best friend?"

"It's a long story and honestly, it's not mine to tell. Parker was planning to talk to Ryder today, I don't know what happened or where he is."

"But his daughter is there with you? Why? How old is she? Did he just abandon a child and left town and no one has heard from him? This is all too crazy and wild, I just can't believe that he would—"

"Brooke!" I said sharply, forcing her to stop before she got herself too worked up and out of control.

"Sorry, this is just a lot to take in."

"That's why I didn't want to tell you over the phone. Gen is Genevieve, his daughter, who is twenty-two years old. She's here with me because she was at Rodney's house while I was there fighting with him about the kids."

"Why was she at Rodney's?"

"Because Genevieve is – was—Gen, his fiancé."

"No. Way."

"Way."

"Okay, you're right. That's a lot to process."

"I told you," I chided.

"Well if you, or *his daughter,* hear from him, please let us know. We're really worried about him with this storm. If he tried to make it to Nashville—"

"I know," I whispered. Neither of us had to finish that sentence. We knew what it meant if he was on the road in the middle of this storm.

"I'll talk to you soon," I assured her before hanging up the phone and walking back into the living room. It was eerily quiet as the kids all stared in horror at the tv screen, no one noticing that I had walked in. I quickly turned my attention to the tv and listened as the screen changed and a live view was broadcasted from the helicopter that was trying to get close enough to the scene of the accident. A semi-truck was laying on its side, several feet down the side of the hill, and beside it was the car it had plowed into, crushing the front to the point where you couldn't recognize what kind of car it was. As the helicopter moved around and changed angles, it gave a quick glimpse of the backside of the car.

Gen's head turned and whipped up to look at me, fear in her eyes when we both recognized the black BMW with the custom license plate. The car had plowed headfirst into an embankment of snow that had already accumulated but according to the news anchor, the driver could not be located. Law enforcement was working on getting a search and rescue team out there as quickly as possible, however, the storm would make it nearly impossible until it passed through. My heart felt like it was about to explode in my chest as I thought about losing the one person who I had finally allowed myself to love.

Fifteen
Parker

I blinked slowly, trying to force myself to wake up. Everything around me was blanketed in white as the icy chill of the snow stung my skin. I knew that I needed to get up and find help, but my body refused to move. It was hard to tell if there was an injury that was preventing me from moving or if I was in some sort of nightmare that I couldn't wake up from. You know the kind that feels so real that you believe you're in it, then you desperately try to escape from whatever demon is trying to kill you before it's too late. As a cold gust of wind whipped past me, I closed my eyes and prayed that the demon was on its way.

Off in the distance, I could swear that I heard the faint sound of people yelling and sirens that were muffled by the snow that was piling up around me. I didn't have to open my eyes to know that the snow was only a few inches away from covering my face and completely burying me. Regardless of how many voices I thought I had heard, no one would reach me in time. It was too late. I let out a shallow breath and allowed myself to succumb to the numbness that had enveloped me.

Sixteen
Sheila

"It's been over twelve hours," I exclaimed as I paced back and forth in front of the kitchen table while Brooke and Ryder watched helplessly. They came right over after we saw Parker's car on the news and the rest of the night had been an emotional blur since then. Gen stuck around and helped me get the kids to bed when they all refused to sleep until they knew that he was safe. After some gentle persuading from Gen and a promise from Brooke that we would wake them up as soon as we heard anything, they all shuffled off down the hall and made their way to bed. Whether or not they were sleeping was a different question that I didn't bother to ask right now.

"They'll find him, Sheila, they have a huge team of people looking for him," Brooke assured me before getting up and pulling the kettle from the stove and serving us all a cup of hot tea. I leaned my head back and ran my hands down my face, saying another prayer that they would find him before it was too late.

I had started to research what was considered 'too late' earlier and was finding plenty of articles that outlined in gory detail what would happen to a body that was left in the snow after x number of hours. I was fully engrossed in an article when Ryder took my phone and refused to give it back two hours ago. My anxiety was at an all-time high as I contemplated every possible scenario and their outcomes. Maybe it wasn't his car, maybe someone else has a car exactly like his with the same custom license plate that was also heading to Nashville. Or maybe he wasn't ejected from the car and thrown into the middle of nowhere on the side of the road in a freaking blizzard that decreased visibility which made it nearly impossible for anyone to find him. Maybe someone was close by when it happened and had already found him and were working on keeping him safe until help could find them. Or maybe he was gone and I was the reason for all of this.

Out of all of the maybes that I had come up with, that last one was the hardest to accept. If I hadn't broken up with Parker this morning then he wouldn't have left in the middle of a deadly snowstorm. I had already beat myself up with all of the *would've, could've, should've* and was driving everyone around me crazy with how obsessive I was getting about it. The problem was that aside from the kids, I've never had anyone in my life who I've loved so much that it killed me to think of living a life that didn't include them. Sure, I loved my parents, as well as Brooke and Ryder, but this was a different kind of love. This was the kind of love that forced its way through an ironclad heart and made a permanent scar to make sure it could never be erased. The kind of love that shattered your soul when you thought about life without ever feeling it again.

Brooke set the cup of tea in front of me on the table and nodded at it. She snuggled up against Ryder and wrapped her arms around his neck while sitting on his lap with his arms around her waist. I knew that they were only trying to comfort each other while we waited for news on Parker but a shot of jealousy coursed through me at what they had.

"Sit down and have some tea," Gen coaxed from the other side of the table, holding her cup in between her hands. I felt my heart skip a beat when she smiled at me, looking just like her dad. With a heavy sigh, I pulled the chair out and sat down. The energy that was flowing through me needed an outlet which resulted in me tapping my foot anxiously underneath the table. Not knowing where he was or if he was safe was worse than anything I had ever gone through with my kids, and they had put me through a lot over the years, especially as they became teenagers.

It was after ten o'clock when we all moved into the living room and sat down to watch the news. The air was thick and filled with desperation as our eyes stayed glued to the tv. Luckily, this snowstorm was unlike anything Stone Creek had seen in over a decade which meant that it took priority and they cut straight to updates on the storm instead of the usual boring stories. I watched as the same weatherman from earlier appeared on the screen, giving updated snowfall totals for each county. My heart started to race when they switched back to the news anchor, hopeful that they would have an update on the accident. I leaned forward and waited.

A few minutes later it went to a commercial and I felt the disappointment start to consume me. Surely, if he had been found, it would have been a top news story. That could only mean one thing… he hadn't been found.

Seventeen
Parker

"Can you open your eyes?"

"Sir, what's your name?"

"Can you hear me?"

"We need you to stay with us, don't you give up on us now."

"Shit, we're losing him!"

"Don't you do this buddy, you've come this far… hold on a little bit longer."

"Starting compressions!"

"Someone get me an update on where his family is. Now!"

"One. Two. Three. Four. Five. Six. Seven. Eight. Nine. Ten.

Eleven. Twelve. Thirteen. Fourteen. Fifteen."

"We need some help over here!"

"Son of a bitch!"

Eighteen
Sheila

"Mommy, can I have pizza for breakfast?"

I opened my eyes to Sally standing in front of me, holding up a slice of cold pizza.

"Sure, just make sure to heat it first. Thirty seconds in the microwave," I mumbled, forcing myself to sit upright in the chair I had fallen asleep in. She walked into the kitchen and tossed it in the microwave without a plate, clearly following the only directions I had given her. I rolled my eyes as I thought about how much simpler it would have been to let her eat the pizza cold but part of me felt like I needed to be a good mom and have her warm it up. Eating cold pizza felt like something you did when you no longer cared about anything and I didn't need my children to know that was how I felt.

By midnight, Ryder and Brooke had decided to go home and promised to call if they heard anything. Gen fell asleep on the couch shortly after they left. The house was quiet and calm which was unusual given all of the kids were home and needed to get ready for school. I was about to get up and head down the hallway to wake them up when I realized that school had to be canceled from the storm. The storm that had kept us up all night worrying about Parker. The storm that possibly took the only man I have ever loved.

Sally waited patiently at the microwave, standing on her tiptoes to watch as the slice of pizza spun around in circles. Once I heard it beep, I quickly yelled to remind her to use a spatula to get it out of the microwave so she didn't burn herself. She laughed and peeked around the wall, waving it in her hand at me. I smiled and leaned back in my chair, feeling my spirits lifted with her sweet personality.

I picked up the remote and turned the volume up enough to hear the news while Gen and the other kids slept. Nothing new had been reported about the storm other than a handful of accidents that had happened in town. The list of school and business closings ran across the bottom of the screen before it switched to a story about a local charity that was hosting a bake sale next week to raise money for the local church. I could feel the tension radiating across the back of my neck and shoulders. My body ached from sleeping in the chair and desperately needed to be up and moving to get some of the blood flowing through it again.

I stood up and reached above me, feeling the glorious relief as I pushed harder and stretched as long as I could. The tension started to alleviate a little as I rubbed my hand along my neck and rolled it. I was bending over, reaching for my toes to stretch my legs when I heard a phone vibrating on the coffee table. I shot straight up and grabbed it, noticing it was Gen's at the same time that her eyes fluttered open. Without saying a word I pushed it toward her, holding my breath as she took it and answered it.

"Yes, this is Genevieve," she paused and waited, nervously chewing her fingernail. "Yes, I'll be right there. Thank you so much for calling."

She hung up the phone then jumped up and smiled at me.

"They found him! He's at the Cedar Bay Hospital. The officer couldn't give me any details on how he's doing but at least now we know where to find him."

"Oh my God, that's incredible," I said breathlessly. My fingers trembled as they hovered over my trembling lips as I tried to keep myself from crying.

"Do you think someone can come watch the kids while you go with me to the hospital?"

I pulled my head back in surprise and looked at her.

"You want me to go with you? What if he doesn't want to see me?"

She reached out and grabbed my hands, holding onto them as she spoke.

"Of course I want you to go with me. I couldn't imagine going with anyone other than the woman who is head over heels in love with my dad. You need to be there. And more importantly, I need you to be there with me… Will you come?"

"Yes!" I squealed and squeezed her hands. I quickly called my mom and asked her to come watch the kids before calling Brooke and Ryder with the update. Ten minutes later, I was putting on my shoes while saying goodbye to the kids and my mom before rushing out the door to jump in Ryder's new truck. Cedar Bay was only an hour away but the snow and ice hadn't been cleared in that area yet which meant that it might slow us down getting there. Ryder had offered to drive us so we didn't have to take two vehicles and since he had recently bought a new truck that he wanted to test out in the bad weather.

The drive to the hospital was quiet. Either we were all too nervous to talk, or we were too tired to bother. I was thankful and relieved that Gen wanted me to be there and prayed that Parker felt the same way when he saw me. There was a lot that I needed to explain to him but that would happen later. For now, I just needed to know that he was alive and okay. Until then, nothing else mattered.

Nineteen
Parker

"Can you tell me your name?"

"Parker Hudson," I croaked, my throat dry and sore after having the tube pulled out of it. The older man with white hair nodded and jotted something down on the clipboard he was holding in his hand.

"Do you know what day it is?" He pulled his brows together doubtfully and waited.

"I don't have any idea. Sunday? Tuesday?" I shrugged my shoulders before remembering that I was wearing a brace around my arm and that the doctor had confirmed that I had fractured my clavicle, amongst other things.

"That was a hard one, sorry," he mumbled and made an additional note before setting the clipboard down on the counter behind him and setting the pen on top. He turned to look at me, his hands folded in his lap as if he was bracing himself for delivering bad news.

"Do you remember what happened? Why you're in the hospital?"

"I was heading back to Nashville and got caught in a snowstorm. I looked down for half a second to turn the heater up and when I looked up, a semi had lost control and plowed right into me. The car spun off the road but I don't remember much after that. Only that I woke up in the hospital."

He nodded and pulled a piece of loose paper from underneath the clipboard.

"According to the police, the impact of the collision with the semi was enough to eject you from the vehicle minutes before the car hit a tree. Luckily, the car hit the tree with enough force that it knocked it over and into the powerlines which was how the rescue crews were able to find you. It took them a little bit of time to get to you because of the storm but the tree led them right to you. I would say that you had quite a bit of luck on your side or a guardian angel looking after you because not many people survive being in the bitter cold that long. We're going to keep you for a few days for monitoring but if everything looks good by Wednesday, we'll go ahead and release you."

"Sounds good, thanks, Doc."

He smiled and patted the table beside me before grabbing his clipboard and walking out the door. I had already seen a handful of nurses and doctors since I had "woken up" and each of them gushed about how lucky I was to still be alive. How I must be some sort of living angel, put here for a divine purpose. I couldn't wrap my head around the details of what happened because everything kept going back to one thing—Sheila.

Twenty
Sheila

The walk through the hospital felt like it took forever and everyone we stopped to ask for help was completely useless. Unfortunately, Gen didn't get anything from the police officer other than that Parker had been taken to Cedar Bay Hospital. We didn't know if he was in the emergency room, the ICU, or somewhere else. It was almost like the officer didn't care about whether she needed that information and I imagined that he was given an update at some point before he called her, yet he treated it as something on his to-do list. Call the family of the man who miraculously survived in the freezing cold for over twelve hours—check.

We walked quickly, trying to find our way around the hospital to the welcome desk. They would be able to look him up in their system and send us on our way. Ryder had parked on the east side of the hospital which shouldn't have been a problem, other than it planted us square in the middle of their radiology and imaging departments. It felt like a ghost town as we wandered the hallways, feeling like we were in some sort of blinding white corn maze. My stomach growled at the smell of the cafeteria food and I knew we were getting closer.

As the hallway came to an end, forming a T, we stopped to look at each other to see which way we should go. It was odd that there weren't any signs up to point us in the right direction but then again there was a fresh coat of paint on the walls which would explain the headache I was starting to get. I moved my head back and forth, trying to find the smell of food. It was stronger to my left so I nodded in that direction and took off walking in search of help.

The hallway continued a few feet before it opened up into a circle with a welcome desk in the middle. I felt my shoulders relax, thankful that we could finally stop this wild goose chase. I made my way over and smiled as I waited for the woman to finish her phone call. She was an attractive woman, probably close to my age but I doubted that she had four children given how perky her boobs were in the tight low-cut sweater she was wearing. Self-consciously, I glanced down at mine and realized that I hadn't bothered to change out of the Pink Floyd t-shirt I had thrown on last night before I fell asleep on the couch. Though my boobs were big, they weren't perky like hers, and this t-shirt did nothing to scream sex-appeal if anyone was looking.

I started panicking, wondering if I should have cleaned up better before we came so that I looked good for Parker when she hung up the phone and smiled at us. Now wasn't the time to worry about how I looked. I knew better than that and felt silly for even thinking about it in the first place. I was nervous to see Parker given how things had ended between us, but I seriously doubted that he would use my current appearance as a basis on whether to talk to me about what had happened.

"How can I help you?" she asked, her voice smooth and sexy like she should be answering a phone-sex line instead of working at the hospital. I bet she would make good money with her voice without having to try. Maybe she does it on the side and she was finishing a call when we walked up. She had blushed and looked away, pulling the mouthpiece of her headset closer to her body as she tucked her chin to her shoulder.

"We're here to see Parker Hudson," Gen explained while I was lost in thought. "The Stone Creek police department said that he was brought here after they found him in the woods."

"Oh! Yes! The Clark Kent looking guy," she gushed excitedly. "Let me see where he is, last I knew they had rushed him to the emergency room." She lowered her head and began typing quickly on the keyboard in front of her. Her freshly manicured nail tapped impatiently on the top of the mouse while she waited for the screen to load the results. "It looks like he's been moved to the tenth floor, room 1028."

"Thank you, we appreciate your help," Ryder said and knocked on the top of the desk a few times before turning around and leading Brooke to the elevators.

"No problem. The nurses and I look forward to giving him

our well wishes soon now that I know he's been moved from the ER," she purred and locked eyes with me. I pulled my head back in surprise, my fist balled at my side when I felt Gen link her arm in mine and pull me away.

"She's not worth it," she whispered as we trailed behind Ryder and Brooke. "I know that I haven't *known* my dad for long, but I feel like I can honestly say that he would *NEVER* go for a woman like that."

I felt the anger and jealousy still pushing through me as I toyed with the idea of going back and punching her perfectly inflated boob to see if I could deflate it. It would delay me seeing Parker by a few minutes, but it would be worth it to knock Malibu Barbie down a peg or two.

"I've known Parker for over ten years and while I *didn't* know that he had a daughter, I can confirm that he would run away from a woman like that. Pretty much every man I know would."

He turned and winked at me over his shoulder as the elevator dinged and the doors slid open. We piled in, and I tried to fight the laughter that was tickling the back of my throat. I lifted my hand to my mouth and stared at the numbers on the wall, the tickle getting stronger. My eyes shifted to the numbers above the door and I watched as each one lit up with each floor we passed. We were almost to the tenth floor and I could feel the urge to burst into laughter getting stronger. I couldn't tell if it was a nervous reaction or simply a coping mechanism for everything that I had recently been through but suddenly the walls of the damn broke and everything came flooding out.

My body shook as I laughed hysterically, reaching over to grab the rail on the side of the wall as I snorted with each breath I tried to take in. Tears were rolling down my face while everyone stared at me in confusion.

"I'm sorry," I gasped, waving my hand in the air to try to dismiss what was happening. "Just ignore me, I'm fine," I snorted and started laughing again. Soon the laughter was contagious and everyone was wiping tears from their eyes as the doors opened to the tenth floor. We scooted off the elevator and popped into the family waiting area so I could try to get myself together. I was starting to get control again, forcing myself to take deep breaths as my sides hurt from laughing so hard. I couldn't remember the last time that I had *really* laughed at something.

"Are you sure you're okay?" Brooke asked, running a hand under her eye to wipe away the eyeliner that had started to smear.

"Yeah, I'm fine," I laughed. "I was so caught up in being angry at that woman that I had seriously thought about running back and punching her in the boob." I lowered my head and started laughing again, the replay of the image I had conjured up replaying in my mind.

"I wouldn't say that she didn't have it coming," Gen joked and leaned against the wall, her hands planted behind her butt.

"I don't even know where that idea came from. I've never had the urge to punch someone in the boob just because they were being flirty about a guy I liked."

"Well, love will do that to you," Brooke sighed and glanced up at Ryder.

"So you're telling me that love leads to having terrible ideas?" I put my hands on my hips and narrowed my eyes at her. I was playing but also stalling now that I knew we would be seeing Parker in a few minutes and I would have to face what happened between us and that I was the reason he was here to begin with.

"I wouldn't worry too much about it." She pursed her lips and shook her head.

"Why's that?" I frowned.

"Because you already have terrible ideas," she laughed, followed by Ryder. He offered a sympathetic smile as I glared at him with daggers in my eyes.

"I DO NOT have terrible ideas. When was the last time I had a terrible idea?" I asked, hands still on my hips. Brooke smiled coyly at me before she grabbed Ryder's hand and started walking down the hallway, forcing me to follow.

"When you wanted to skip and drink wine," she said over her shoulder as I felt Gen walking beside me. "And your worst one is thinking you can stall in the waiting room to keep from having to go in and talk to Parker."

I stayed quiet, not bothering to answer since anything I would have said would be a lie. Brooke knew me better than I knew myself so I should have seen that one coming. We walked down the hallway, ignoring the nurses that were busy at the station off to the right. I slowed my pace when I saw the room numbers getting closer, my heart skipping a beat as we got to his.

"Are you ready?" Ryder asked Gen and me as we stood pale as a ghost in front of the door, holding hands. I sucked in a deep breath and waited as Ryder opened the door.

Twenty One
Parker

"I meant it when I said the last person I wanted to see was you," I mumbled as I rolled onto my side, ignoring the person who had opened the door. I closed my eyes and tried to force myself to sleep, the inability to feel warm keeping me awake. No matter how hard I tried I couldn't escape the icy chill that seemed to still linger inside my body. It was as if my veins had been frozen and the blood inside was slowly trickling along, too cold to get where it needed to go.

"Well aren't you a peach?" Ryder joked.

I whipped my head around and looked, excited to see Ryder standing there with Brooke, Genevieve, and Sheila. My heart started beating wildly in my chest, my hands anxious to reach out and touch Sheila. To make sure she was real and that I wasn't dreaming of her or having another hallucination like I had when I was in the snow.

"I thought you were someone else," I mumbled, trying to explain myself. My eyes stayed glued to Sheila as I watched how she nervously shied away and tried to hide behind everyone else. She kept her head down and studied the ugly tile on the floor to keep from looking at me while she pulled at a loose string on the Pink Floyd t-shirt she sleeps in. I found myself smiling at the memory of her waking up in that same t-shirt on New Year's morning after we had spent the night together. She apologized for her faded, worn-out t-shirt but I loved her in it. It was perfectly Sheila. No-fuss and no high maintenance to make her look beautiful. She could wear a garbage bag and still look sexy.

"How are you feeling?" Ryder asked as he stepped closer, Brooke right behind him. I tried to catch Sheila's eye, but she continued to avoid me. I glanced over at Genevieve and while she didn't avoid looking at me, she was staring out the window with tears in her eyes.

"I'm alive, so I'll take that," I joked, instantly regretting it when I saw the reactions on their faces. "Sorry, that was a bad attempt at lightening the mood." I shook my head and ran a hand through my hair. "I feel like shit but at least there's nothing serious that they're worried about. Right now I'm resting and drinking plenty of warm fluids while they run an IV through me. I was lucky that I landed in an area that had a lot of leaves piled up which added some insulation. Thankfully, I was dressed in plenty of layers that helped save me."

"I still can't believe it," Ryder shook his head and stood

next to me. "I'm so thankful that you're okay."

I could hear his voice crack and knew that this was hard for him. I reached up and gently patted his arm with the little strength that I had. His hand found mine and patted it in return before I let it fall beside me, the energy to keep it up there too much for me to handle. I wanted to reach out and pull Genevieve and Sheila over to me to make sure that they were okay, but I was scared as shit to even talk to them. Everything was new and I had no idea how to tread these new waters with a daughter who I just recently reconnected with and a woman who I was head-over-heels in love with. I wasn't the kind of guy who did love so I had NO IDEA how to handle this.

"Gen, did you want to come see your dad?" Brooke asked softly, doing all of the work for me as if she knew I was struggling with what to do.

She turned and looked at me, tears staining her cheeks as she nodded yes. I held my arms open for her, hoping she would accept the invitation. She rushed over and bent down, wrapping her arms gently around me as we hugged. I couldn't remember the last time I hugged her but something told me that it was when I said goodbye to her fifteen years ago. She trembled in my arms, her tears dripping onto my shoulder. I hugged her as tight as I could with what strength I had left. A few minutes later, she pulled away and wiped her face with the back of her hand.

"Are you really okay?" she asked before sitting on the edge of the bed after Brooke and Ryder had taken the two seats off to the side by the window.

"Yes, sweetheart, I'm really okay."

"I was so scared that I was going to lose you," she whispered, fighting back more tears.

"You will never lose me again, I promise you that. I will always be here for you and I'll use my superhuman powers to escape death as many times as I need," I teased before adding, "but I really hope that there won't be any more near-death experiences in my future. I barely dodged this bullet, I can't imagine that I would be that lucky a second time around."

Everyone chuckled except for Sheila. I hadn't forgotten that she was there. I intended to give her time, allow her to feel comfortable before I tried to talk to her. I knew things were bad with how we left them this morning, but I prayed that she would be open to talking it out and seeing if we could work through everything together. I didn't care anymore about whether she let me be a part of her life with Rodney in the way that I thought I needed. I was convinced that she was delicate and fragile, that she needed protecting. But I was completely wrong about that. She was fierce and strong, the kind of woman who didn't need a knight in shining armor to come save the day. This was probably a good thing since I couldn't remember where I had stored my shining armor…

The room grew quiet and an awkward silence prevailed. I wasn't the only one who had noticed that Sheila was still hiding in the corner of the room as Brooke kept leaning to the side, trying to get her attention before not-so-subtly nodding in my direction for her to come talk to me. I was about to say something funny to draw her attention over to me but before I could think of what to say, the door opened and the one woman I *didn't* want to see walked in.

She stood in the doorway, surprise on her face as she looked around, her face recently touched up with a new layer of powder and a fresh coat of red lipstick. Her black hair was neatly tucked behind her ear, each strand perfectly in place.

"Well, hello darlings," she purred as she squared her shoulders and ran her hands down the front of her dry-clean-only navy blue blazer that matched the pinstripe satin shirt underneath. "It looks like we have company, dear," she said crisply as her eyes narrowed at me in disapproval.

Twenty Two
Sheila

If I wanted to crawl in a corner and hide when I thought about seeing Parker, this woman made me want to crawl under a bed and pull the blankets down over me so she would never find me. Everything about her demanded attention from her salon colored hair to her overly priced heels that probably cost more than my monthly mortgage payment. Her smile appeared forced, even through the layers of Botox that was already pulling her skin tight across her thin, angular face. We all stared on, in confusion, as Parker worked his jaw back and forth, glaring at her. I stepped to the side, moving out of the way as the door opened again and a man walked in.

He looked like he was ready to go play golf at some ritzy country club with his pristine white sweater wrapped around his broad shoulders. His navy blue pants paired perfectly with the white polo that was neatly tucked in and adorned by a thin black belt. He stood next to the woman and attempted to wrap an arm around her shoulder before her side-eyed glare made him rethink it. He lowered his arm by his side and stood up straight, more rigid than I had ever seen anyone. As I looked at the power couple before me, I couldn't help but wonder if their outfits were strategically matched with navy and white, or if it was purely coincidental.

"I see you have company," the man commented, barely moving his head as he glanced around the room.

"Nothing gets by you, Dad," Parker mumbled and shifted in the bed. Genevieve was standing beside him, fiddling with her fingers while avoiding the penetrating stare the woman was giving her.

"That's no way to speak to your parents," the woman attempted to lecture, only to get an eye-roll in return.

"Everyone, these are my parents. Willa and Bradly Hudson." He nodded in their direction.

"*Doctor* Willa Hudson," she corrected.

"My *mother* is a retired Oncologist who used to work at this hospital. Now she serves on the board of directors which is how she was informed that I was here, after I was brought in." He looked from Ryder to me, an apologetic look on his face.

"Well, it's not like you would have bothered to call and tell us yourself. Unlike your *friends*. I guess we see where we rate these days." Her tone was harsh.

"Gee, I'm sorry mom. I guess I didn't think to call and tell you that I was laying in the snow after being ejected from my car when a semi came crashing into me. I was barely alive when someone found me, and they rushed me to the hospital. But how careless and selfish of me not to call you the minute that I woke up." He worked his jaw back and forth again, the tension in his shoulders visible from across the room. I wanted to walk over and hold him, protect him from this woman, and promise to never leave him again.

"And just for the record, I didn't call my friends to tell them I was here. I'm glad that they're here, but I don't know how they found out that I had been in an accident or that I was at Cedar Bay."

"An officer called me with the update. I had called them asking for information after we saw the accident on the news, and I recognized your car. Sheila and I had been calling them throughout the night, asking for an update, but they didn't have one. I got a call this morning, and we rushed right over," Genevieve explained calmly.

"And you are…" Willa's eyes narrowed in at her as if she was trying to figure out why she looked familiar.

"I'm Genevieve." She looked nervously at Parker, unsure of whether she should say more. It was obvious that Willa and Bradly had no idea who she was. Willa's eyes popped open in surprise when she heard the name, quickly looking at Parker for an answer to a question that she hadn't asked.

"She's my daughter," he said proudly. He reached up and squeezed her hand, never taking his eyes off of his mother.

"Her name is Genevieve?" Willa questioned quietly, her attitude from a few minutes ago already starting to dissipate.

"Yes. Amy and I named her Genevieve after—"

"I know who she was named after," Willa bit out, cutting him off. "I guess I shouldn't be surprised that you would name your child after her given that you didn't bother to tell me that you *had a child.* How old are you my dear?" She laced the fake pleasantries on thick enough to smother the entire room.

"I'm twenty-two."

Willa and Bradly exchanged a glance as they calculated the math in their heads then looked back at Parker.

"You had a child when you were eighteen and didn't bother to tell us? You were still living under our roof, under our control—" Willa's voice started to rise.

"Keyword—control. I moved out the second that I turned eighteen and didn't bother looking back. Which also meant that I didn't bother with telling you that I had gotten Amy pregnant or that she was moving to Arkansas to be with her family so they could help her raise the baby. You were already packed and ready to walk out the door on my eighteenth birthday to come start your new life in Cedar Bay so what difference would it have made?" Parker's voice was filled with anger as it rose to the same volume as Willa's. She pulled her shoulders back and tilted her side to look at him, an almost hurt look on her face.

"I can't believe you honestly think that we would have

walked away and not wanted to be there for our grandchild. For you. To help you raise it. Is that why you let Amy take her away to Arkansas?"

"Oh please, Mother. You were barely there for me as a child, why on earth would I think that you would have stuck around and been there to help me raise your grandchild? Amy took her because we both agreed that it was the best thing for the baby. I had no idea what it took to be a good father because I didn't have a good example of parenting while I was growing up."

"That's a terrible thing to say. We gave you everything you could have ever wanted. Plenty of private tutors, summers away at camp—what more could you have wanted?"

The room was silent as we all watched the drama that was unfolding in front of us. Now I understood what Parker meant when we first walked in and he made the comment about being the last person he wanted to see. My heart had dropped out of my chest, and I hung paralyzed in the corner of the room, worried that I had made a terrible mistake by coming. I wasn't completely sure that I hadn't made a mistake or that he did want to see me, but I was pretty confident that the comment was meant for his parents and not any of us.

I studied his dad for a moment and wondered why this entire time he had stayed quiet. He hadn't tried to jump into the conversation at all and if I had to guess, I would say that Willa was controlling with him as well. Hell, she probably picked the outfit he was wearing just so he would have to match her. She didn't seem like the type of woman who easily relinquished control in any aspect of her life.

Parker had been looking down at the floor while his mom spoke, refusing to meet the cold stare that she was giving him. Slowly, he looked up and locked eyes with her.

"Love. Compassion. Empathy. Understanding. Guidance. Parents that actually gave a damn about me as a person and not what I looked like on paper."

My heart shattered for him. We hadn't talked about his past much. He was always tight-lipped about it and now I knew why. I couldn't imagine growing up in a house where I didn't feel loved or wanted by my parents and I made sure that my children never felt that either.

"I think we've had enough excitement for the day, honey. Why don't we let Parker catch up with his friends, and we'll check on him later?" Bradly reached over and gently touched Willa's elbow, turning her away and walking out the door. She stayed silent and held her head high as she left with a smug look on her face.

After the door closed behind them, the tension in the air seemed to evaporate, and everyone let out the breath that they had been holding. It had been uncomfortable, to say the least, but I was more concerned with how Parker was doing than anything else. I looked up at him at the same time that his eyes found me again, and everything in the room felt like it froze in place. No one else was there but the two of us, as we silently said all the things we needed to say to each other. I felt tears prickle my eyes, a sting in my throat as I tried to keep myself from crying.

"You know, I could really use something to drink. Do you

ladies want to go with me to see if we can find a vending machine and give these two a moment to talk?" Ryder asked, grabbing Brooke's hand as they stood up and walked toward the door. Gen's smile spread tightly across her face as she looked at me and gave me a quick hug before leaving. I waited for the sound of the door closing behind them while I thought about what to say. Once we were alone, I took a few steps toward him and stood at the end of the bed, trying to work up the courage to speak.

"Parker, I'm so sorry," I choked out, still fighting the tears back so I could talk. "I never should have ended things with you, and this is all my fault." My head dropped forward in shame as a tear slid down my cheek.

"Sheila, come here," he coaxed and extended his hand to me.

Refusing to lift my head and look at him, I reached out and took his hand. I could feel the tingle I got every time my body touched his, as the butterflies spread right through me. He pulled me closer until I was standing right beside him.

"Sit down next to me, please," he said as he scooted over and made room for me. I glanced down to make sure that his IV was out of the way before I sat on the very edge, only a sliver of my butt cheek actually touching the bed. I could feel his gaze on me, waiting for me to look up at him. When I continued to refuse, he gently reached over and tipped my chin up with his finger.

"You're not the one who needs to apologize, Sheila. I should be apologizing to *you*. I should have never been so aggressive with forcing myself into your life with Rodney, and I'm sorry for putting you in that position to begin with. Our relationship was so new, and I didn't wait for us to define the boundaries before I stepped right over them. I'm so sorry that I pushed you, and I promise that I won't do that again. You have my word."

I saw the emotion in his eyes as his voice cracked toward the end. There was pure honesty and sincerity in every word, something that I had never experienced before. Rodney was the only serious relationship that I had, and I married him knowing that most of what he said was simply what he thought I wanted to hear. It felt weird to hear someone say something that they actually meant.

"You didn't overstep. I should have stopped and thought things through before I rushed out of your hotel room. You were only trying to be helpful and I completely disregarded you and treated you like you were Rodney. I didn't give you the chance to show me that you could be there for me before treating you as if you had somehow already let me down."

I felt like a huge weight had been lifted as we talked things out and cleared the air between us. He rested his arm on my thigh and laced his fingers in between mine.

"Well, if you'll still have me as your boyfriend, I promise to talk to you about things beforehand and to let you guide me on what you want and need. I don't want a relationship like my parents have where my mom orders my dad around. I want us to be equal in everything and for us to support each other. But above everything else, I just want to wake up next to you every morning and see you in this Pink Floyd t-shirt that you love so much," he teased as he reached over and tugged at it.

"This t-shirt has seen me through some tough times… I'm not giving it up any time soon," I warned playfully.

"Good," he said with a laugh. "Because I'm getting quite fond of it. It's almost thin enough that I can get a sneak peek of the goodies if you know what I mean…" He wiggled his eyebrows. I felt my cheeks flush with heat as I quickly dropped his hand and pulled the shirt out to see if it was as see-through as he said. He leaned back and rested his arm above his head, chuckling while he watched me freak out. I reached over and playfully swatted at him before laughing and shaking my head.

"You jerk, you had me worried that I was running around in a slutty shirt," I scolded and narrowed my eyes at him.

"It was worth it to see you get riled up. I missed my feisty little woman."

"Well, the lady at the Welcome Desk downstairs sure took a liking to you—or should I say *Clark Kent*. It doesn't look like you would have any trouble finding another woman if you needed to."

"Clark Kent, huh? Well, I can tell you right now that this superhero only has eyes for you. You're my only Kryptonite."

"Oh my god, that was the cheesiest line I've ever heard." I rolled my eyes and laughed. "And I *married* Rodney!" I laughed harder as his bottom lip jutted out in a fake attempt at pouting.

"I still have to get used to the idea that my girlfriend used to be married to my future son-in-law. I don't think I ever want to know any details from you or from Genevieve about that man. It just creeps me out." He shivered and made a disgusted face.

"I don't think you have to worry about that anymore," I said before realizing that I should let Gen tell him about her and Rodney. My face turned red which he noticed immediately.

"Why not? What happened?"

"It's not for me to tell. Gen can explain it when she gets back," I said passively, hoping that he wouldn't press the issue.

"Am I going to have to go kick his ass? Did he do something to her?"

I looked over my shoulder as the door creaked open and felt relieved when I saw Ryder, Brooke, and Gen coming back in.

"Just in time," I muttered under my breath as I stood up and turned to face them. Parker reached up and pulled me down next to him again, this time facing the same direction. I tried to make sure I wasn't sitting on his IV or any other medical equipment before I allowed myself to snuggle up next to him.

"Do I need to go kick Rodney's ass?" he asked Gen as she sat down on the stool that was under the cabinet by the wall. Her expression changed from panic to confusion before she looked at me for clarification. She shrugged and waited for him to go on.

"Why would you need to kick Rodney's ass?" she replied

with her brows pulled together. She twisted the top on her bottle of water and took a drink. Brooke and Ryder sat down in the seats beside the bed after Brooke handed me a bottle of lemon-flavored iced tea. I mouthed a quick *thank you* to her before returning my attention to Parker and Gen.

"I was talking to Sheila about how weird it was that my girlfriend used to be married to my daughter's current fiancé and she said that I didn't have to worry about that anymore. What happened? Did he do something to you that I need to go kick his ass for?"

Gen giggled and wiped her mouth with the back of her hand after she almost spit out her mouthful of water.

"No, you don't need to go kick his ass because we're no longer together. I decided to break it off with him."

"You broke up with him?"

"Yes," she confirmed with a soft chuckle.

"But not because he was being an asshole to you?"

"Right," she nodded. "Because he was being an asshole to Sheila and I didn't want to be with someone like that."

"He was an asshole to you?" he asked, turning his head to look down at me as I stayed tucked in under his arm.

"He's always an asshole, what's new?" I shrugged.

"I'm gonna—" his voice trailed off, filled with anger.

"Kick his ass?" Ryder offered sarcastically.

"Yeah, right after I get done with you," he pushed back with a smug smile that had all of us laughing.

"Maybe when you're not hooked up to life-saving machines in a hospital, old man." Ryder's eyes lit up with amusement as he continued to poke at him.

"Hey, you're not that far behind me." He raised his eyebrows, looking just like his mom for a second, though I would never tell him that.

"I've still got a few years before I hit the big FOUR. ZERO."

"I'm like a fine wine my friend, I only get better with age." He gently squeezed my shoulders and placed a kiss on top of my head. "I like having you next to me, you warm me up better than any of their so-called *life-saving* treatments," he whispered in my ear. I felt the pride swell inside of me as I pushed myself closer to him, ready to warm him up the best I could.

"So, are we having a big party for the big day? I can make the cake…" Brooke offered excitedly. If there was one thing Brooke loved more than Ryder, it was baking cakes and throwing parties.

"I don't see any reason to," Parker said with a scowl. "It's just another day."

"You just survived a near-death sarcexperience after being ejected from a car and left in the freezing cold for hours. That's something to celebrate so, yes, we are having a party, and yes, I will help you plan it, Brooke." Gen gave Parker a pointed look before folding her arms over her chest.

"Fine, whatever makes you guys happy. Just one request though…"

We all waited silently for him to tell us what it was. Finally, an ornery smile pulled across his face as he said, "Don't you dare invite my parents."

The room was filled with laughter as we all agreed that we wouldn't invite them.

"Can I ask you a question?" Gen asked once the laughter had settled down.

"Sure," Parker said softly.

"Who am I named after?"

It had been on my mind from the moment Willa reacted to the name and I was curious who they had named her after as well. Parker closed his eyes and lowered his head, taking a moment before letting out a gentle breath.

"You're named after your great-grandma. Genevieve was my mother's mom and she practically raised me when my parents weren't around. My mom had a terrible relationship with her mother and she hated that I was so close to her. They were constantly at odds with each other and my mother hated everything about how easy-going and carefree my grandma was. She was the only person that I had growing up that had ever taken the time to show me how to love someone."

He paused for a moment and I could see the emotion on his face as his eyes filled with tears. He quickly tried to blink them away before they spilled over and down his face.

"I had told her about you when your mom and I first found out that she was pregnant. She understood my decision to let Amy take you to Arkansas and she supported us. After you were born, she and I drove down to meet you and she fell madly in love with you. You looked up at her with these big, beautiful eyes and wrapped your fingers around hers, and you bonded quicker than anything I had ever seen. We decided to honor her by giving you her name."

"Honor her?" Gen asked in a whisper.

"She was very sick and passed shortly after you were born. Stage four colon cancer."

My head felt dizzy as I pulled all of the pieces together.

"But your mom…" I said, letting my thoughts trail off into thin air.

"Is an Oncologist?" he offered, finishing my sentence. I nodded sadly, knowing where this was going.

"She was one of the best but unfortunately, even the best couldn't save my grandma."

"I'm so sorry," I choked out, the emotional toll of the day finally catching up with me. Everyone else murmured their condolences as well.

"Thank you. I miss her every single day and I constantly

feel the void of not having her here when I have exciting news that I want to share or when I'm having a bad day and need someone to talk to. But I know that she's always there in one way or another, and yesterday, I sat and talked to her for a while as I waited in the snow for them to rescue me."

We all stayed quiet, unsure of what to say.

"I know that everyone thinks that I'm crazy, and the doctors have all explained that I was likely having hallucinations in my altered mental state as my body tried to compensate for the extreme hypothermia. But I remember her very clearly and whether it was me on the brink of death, getting to visit with an angel, or simply a hallucination to keep me calm during a terrifying moment in my life—it doesn't matter to me. I'm just thankful that I had her with me to get me through it. Her strength is the reason that I'm here. It's always been what has pushed me forward and guided me in life."

"It's such an honor to share her name and I hope that I can live a life that would have made her proud," Gen said as the tears rolled down her face.

"You've already done that," Parker assured her. "You make all of us proud and I see so much of her in you."

I closed my eyes and laid my head on his chest, listening to the beautiful sound of his heart beating. For once in my life, I finally felt like I had everything I could possibly want.

Epilogue - Fourth of July
Sheila

"Be careful with that sparkler, Thomas," I warned. "If you catch your sister's hair on fire again, you won't get any allowance for the rest of the year."

"Come on mom, it was just the one time and it all grew back," he whined and held his sparkler an inch too close to his sister's hair. Sally had just turned thirteen and was determined to look more grown-up than she needed to which meant we were in the stage of her trying every hair and beauty product that she could get her hands on. This week it was hairspray.

"Try me and see what happens." I tilted my head and placed my hand on my hip, my warning look penetrating past him to Rodney as he walked around the corner carrying a plate covered in foil and a blonde woman practically on his hip.

"I would do as you're told, son, your mama doesn't look like she's playing," Rodney called over his shoulder to Thomas who rolled his eyes and took off to chase the other neighborhood boys who were now running in circles with their sparklers. I don't know if it was the long holiday weekend or the amount of sugar that they had already consumed from the other houses during the street party, but these kids were out of control today.

"You know my look well," I teased with wide eyes, reaching for the plate that he extended to me.

"I've seen it a time or two," he said playfully, lowering his head and tilting it to the side where the blonde was still standing. I took a moment to take her in, relieved that she at least appeared to be closer to our age than Gen was. Her blonde hair looked dry and brittle, a good sign that she wasn't young and blessed with naturally healthy hair. Nor did she seem like a high-maintenance girl that was going to blow all of his money on deep conditioning treatments.

Brooke had given me a gift card to the local salon for my birthday, and I spent the day doing just that—getting my hair cut and colored, as well as the deep conditioning that everyone swore by. By the time I left, I felt like a new woman, and I considered which child I might give up to free up some funds each month so I could keep going back for that luxury treatment. Parker was so impressed by it that we had the hottest sex that night, followed by another round of intense love making the next morning. I was lost in thought, thinking about the night of seven orgasms, when the woman quietly tried to clear her throat to get Rodney's attention. I snapped out of my trance and smiled at her.

"Hi, I'm Sheila," I said as I extended my hand to her. She shook it with an impressive grip—not too hard and not flimsy like most people when they saw my petite frame.

"I'm Lizzie, Rodney's girlfriend," she said shyly. They looked at each other and shrugged, reminiscent of two teenagers going on their first date together.

"It's nice to meet you."

We made small talk for a few minutes before they made their way over to the area where the kids were playing with the sparklers. I glanced over to make sure that Thomas hadn't caught anything on fire before checking on the other kids. Oliver was sitting on the front lawn talking with Ryder and Brooke while Megan was cozied up next to her boyfriend on the tailgate of his truck as they watched the kids play. Sally was now the one chasing Thomas, which wasn't unusual in the least.

I set the plate down that Rodney and Lizzie had brought, pulling off the foil to the plate of red, white, and blue Rice Krispy treats. They were arranged in different sizes and laid out on the plate in the shape of a flag. I smiled when I thought about how much Rodney had changed in the last six months and how far we had come since the day Gen broke up with him. While he made a few attempts to get her to take him back, he didn't obsess about it like he usually would have. Instead, he stopped drinking and started coming around more to spend time with the kids.

Parker had warmed up to him after they were forced to spend more time together once he officially moved in with me. At first, I was stressed and worried that I would have to walk on eggshells to keep the peace in the house between the two, but thankfully Parker was a mature adult who handled himself around Rodney without sinking to his level of immaturity. The next thing I knew, I came home one day from picking up a pizza and found both of them sitting on the couch watching football while Rodney waited for the kids to get their things ready to go to his house.

Six months had changed a lot, and I felt the void of having Gen in Arkansas with her mom. I knew that Amy was sick and that Gen wanted to be there to help take care of her, but I also worried that she was giving up so much of her own life to do so. I also worried about Parker and how he would take it watching his daughter take care of her dying mother after having been the one to take care of his dying grandmother, who was like a mother to him. Things were hard and stressful, but Gen stayed in touch with us. We looked forward to our weekly phone calls with her.

I looked down and checked the time, making sure that we didn't miss tonight's call. I wanted her to come to town for the holiday weekend since it was the annual Fourth of July street party tonight and Parker's birthday party tomorrow night. Unfortunately, she couldn't get away at the last minute, and her stepdad needed her help while he worked a double shift. I felt strong arms wrap around my waist and grinned as I laid my head against Parker's chest while he held me from behind.

Everyone was distracted by the fireworks that were starting now that the sun had set and the sky was dark. His hands slowly worked their way up from my stomach and squeezed my breasts before rubbing them with the palms of his hands.

"You better be careful, someone might catch us," I warned, not giving a damn whether anyone caught us or not. His hands were magical and my body craved his touch.

"Well, I just happen to know a place we can go," he offered seductively, nipping at my ear before pulling away and leading me away from the crowd. There was just enough light between the houses for us to safely sneak back behind the old wood shed that sat in the corner of the backyard. I could see everyone clearly but felt excited to know that no one could see us. Unless they were right in front of us, no one would know we were back here.

Parker leaned against the shed and pulled me against him, covering my mouth with his as his hands wrapped around the back of my neck. I ran my hands up his chest, digging my nails into his skin just enough to get the reaction I wanted out of him as he growled under his breath. He pulled away and nudged my head to the side as he started working its way down my neck, kissing the spots that he knew turned me on. My breathing got heavier as the ache between my thighs started to throb.

"Tell me what you want," he whispered, his hand roaming over my breast before dropping down to my shorts and cupping my pussy. I hissed in response, my back arching instinctively.

"I want you to fuck me," I panted breathlessly.

"Where?"

"Here."

"Here?"

"Now."

He growled low in my ear before spinning me around wrapping his arm around my waist. I reached down and unbuttoned my denim jeans, pulling them down to my thighs as quickly as I could as I heard him unzip his pants. He gently pushed me forward so I was bent slightly at the waist as he slid himself inside of me, my pussy already wet and ready for him. I spread my legs apart as far as I could, letting my shorts slide down a little, as he thrust inside of me. My hand grabbed onto the side of the shed to hold myself up while I bit back the urge to scream his name and draw attention to us. He continued to slam into me from behind, while I watched our neighbors stuff their faces with hotdogs and corn on the cob.

I could feel myself getting closer as I reached down and rubbed my clit roughly, trying to bring myself to climax at the same time he had his release. He chuckled and placed his hand over mine, working his fingers in the same rhythm as I clenched my pussy around his thick cock and drained the orgasm out of both of us. His hand held me in place as my body went limp, completely satisfied, and relaxed.

"You gotta be quiet, I'm pretty sure Mrs. Woodcock heard you moaning at one point. She turned to look for the noise before a firework grabbed her attention again," he teased as he pulled out and slid himself back inside of his shorts. I giggled as I pulled mine up and buttoned them before adjusting my shirt to make sure I didn't have anything showing that shouldn't be. The last thing my kids or anyone else needed to see was their mom coming from the dark backyard with a nipple hanging out.

We finished up and snuck into the back door of the house, ready to go clean up and pretend like we had been inside all along. When we walked inside, I didn't expect to see anyone in the house so I jumped and screamed before realizing that it was Gen.

"Gen! What are you doing here?!" I rushed over to hug her before Parker could beat me to it.

"Sean's parents came into town this weekend and they offered to look after my mom while I came down to celebrate dad's birthday," she explained excitedly between hugs.

"That's so great! Why didn't you tell me earlier that you were coming?" I asked as I reached up and tucked a stray hair behind my ear. There was something thin and hard beneath my fingers and I started to freak out that it was a bug when I pulled it out and saw that it was just a twig from the tree that hung over the shed. I quickly tossed it behind me into the sink, hoping she hadn't noticed.

"I wanted to surprise you guys," she said with a sly smile. "And it looks like I did just that…"

"We were just watching the fireworks before coming inside to get more chips," I lied as quickly as I could.

"Sure you were," she teased.

"It's good to see you," Parker said as he wrapped an arm

around her shoulder and walked with her to the front
door. He turned to give me a sexy smile. I could hear him
asking about her new job before the door closed behind
them. I turned and held onto the sink, shaking my head at
how Parker and I almost got caught worse than Gen just
assuming she knew what we were doing. I looked down at
the twig and giggled, never feeling so young and free before
in my life.

Acknowledgements

Thank you so much for all of the love, excitement, and support everyone has poured into this book. I love creating stories that people are excited for and this one was no exception. A huge thank you to all of the bloggers who eagerly waited for this book and jumped on the opportunity to read an ARC of it as soon as it was available. Your support means so much to me!

My continued love and gratitude goes out to my wonderful alpha readers, Chelsea and Azucena. You ladies are amazing and I hope you always know your worth. Thank you for always being by my side and helping me through each book.

Tillie, thank you for making the time to for me to edit this book when you had your hands full with a million other things. I appreciate your support and dedication.

To my parents and sister, thank you guys for your support with another book! I love that you're so eager to tell people about my books and encourage them to check them out.

Richard, thank you for all of your help. From being a wonderful husband, to an amazing dad, to a rockstar editor/graphic designer/ formatter— you do it all without complaining. I couldn't imagine a world without you in it and I will forever be grateful to you.

To my sweet girls, believe in yourself and never allow anyone to create any doubt in your mind. You can do ANYTHING.
To the readers- thank you so much for reading Sheila and Parker's story. I know you have millions of books to choose from and I'm so honored that you chose mine. Hopefully this book gave you a couple of hours of enjoyment as you escaped into another world, and that you laughed along with Sheila as she stumbled through parts of it.

About the Author

Samantha lives in the southwest with her husband and two small children after abandoning her childhood dream of living in a cabin in Colorado when she found that she couldn't afford to live there and was deathly allergic to the woods. When she's not writing she's usually spouting off sarcastic remarks while drinking wine out of a coffee mug to look like a functional adult while chasing down her toddlers. She enjoys spending time with her family, watching reruns of FRIENDS, and the 24/7 flow of coffee that can be found in her veins. Be sure to follow her on social media for updates on what she's working on.

You can find her here:

Facebook: https://www.facebook.com/AuthorSamanthaBaca

Instagram: https://instagram.com/author_samantha_baca

Goodreads: http://www.goodreads.com/authorsamanthabaca

Facebook Reader Group:
https://www.facebook.com/groups/2945710968775398/

Webpage: https://authorsamanthabaca.wordpress.com

Newsletter: http://eepurl.com/g0NcSj

Other Books By Samantha Baca

'Til Death Do Us Part (Haven Brook Book 1)
https://www.amazon.com/dp/B087TG2JZV

The Cradle Will Fall (Haven Brook Book 2)
https://www.amazon.com/dp/B08GBZG3HS

The Ties That Bind (Haven Brook Book 3)
https://www.amazon.com/dp/B08P4281BC

A Very Haven Christmas (Haven Brook Book 3.5)
https://www.amazon.com/dp/B08PY9R1TP

Five Steps Ahead (Dark Shadows Book 1)
http://www.amazon.com/dp/B08CMXGL9G

Finding Love In Apartment 2C
https://www.amazon.com/dp/B08JHBFQH8

Chocolate Covered Mistletoe
https://www.amazon.com/dp/B08PPYSHCT